GOOD 2 GO

Money Make Me Cum

ERNEST MORRIS

Good2Go Publishing

Money Make Me Cum

Written by Ernest Morris
Cover Design: Davida Baldwin
Typesetter: Mychea
ISBN: 978-1-947340-02-2
Copyright ©2017 Good2Go Publishing
Published 2017 by Good2Go Publishing
7311 W. Glass Lane • Laveen, AZ 85339
www.good2gopublishing.com
https://twitter.com/good2gobooks
G2G@good2gopublishing.com
www.facebook.com/good2gopublishing
www.instagram.com/good2gopublishing

ACKNOWLEDGEMENTS

First and foremost, I have to thank God once again for keeping me focused long enough to produce another novel.

Second, I would like to thank all my readers for supporting me and keeping me motivated to bring you into my world whether it be fiction or nonfiction.

A special shout-out goes to my homie EDWARD MOSES. Keep your head up, and be safe. Time heals all wounds, bro, and you're a fighter. Trust me, I know!

Shout out to my brothers: Kevin (Chubb) and Sedric (Walid) Morris. Rasheed, Frank, and Maurice Turner.

Thanks to Googd2Go Publishing for continuing to believe in me.

Shout out to Leneek, Nakisha, Brandi, Kendra, Meana, Le'Shea, Shayana, Sahmeer, Demina, Bo, Dee, Tysheeka, Tasha, Barry, Richard (RIP), Aliyah aka Fish (RIP), Queanna, Dwunna Theresa, Loveana, Ty, Peanut, Janell, Trina, Markida, Sharon, Aneatra, Phyllis, Eric, Andre, Eddie, Tamara, Janay, Bey, Yahnise, Nyia, Pamela, Symiya, Mira, Alisha, Shannon, Dee Dee, Damien, Nafeese, Kenya, Nyeemah, My Cheesecake Family, etc. Anyone else that I forgot to mention, it wasn't intentional, but thank you also. I've done it again!!!!

ONE

"Tamara, get up and get ready for school. I told you about staying up late on a school night. I will be working late today, so your father will be there to pick you up," her mother said, standing in the doorway.

Tamara sat up, moving her hair from over her face, then sucked her teeth at her mom. She hated being alone with her stepfather because he was too creepy. At age sixteen, she was the total opposite of her mother. Her mom was beautiful, with a body that resembled Kim K's. She was a dime to most men, while to others, she was a twelve. She always wore clothes that were revealing and left nothing to the imagination. Tamara, on the other hand, was the nerdy, boyish type that wore baggy clothes all the time because she didn't like people staring at her.

"He's not my father, and why can't I just come to your job and wait for you?"

"For one, you're only sixteen, and I don't want you around those kind of people. Now hurry up and get yourself together so we can get out of here," she replied, leaving Tamara to get dressed.

After getting ready, Tamara made it to school just as the late bell rang. She rushed to class trying not to be late. All the girls snickered and whispered to each other as she walked

past and took a seat at her desk.

"Nice of you to join us, Ms. Moses. We're on page 218 in your textbook," her teacher said, giving her a sarcastic look.

Tamara quickly opened her book and joined in on the discussion. She gave the snickering girls a "don't fuck with me" look, then smiled to herself. They liked picking on her for dressing unattractively, but she ignored them. The class clown was some dude name Ed. He was a small-time drug dealer that loved attention and would do anything to get it. He sat directly behind Tamara.

"Why you never wear girly clothes?" he whispered in her ear. "I bet your butt is too small."

"Don't worry about my ass," she replied.

Tamara had a crush on him, but of course she never told him. He could have any girl he wanted, so why would he want her? Ed saw the teacher staring at him and sat back in his chair. His boys were smiling the whole time. After class, everyone headed toward the door.

"Ms. Moses, let me speak with you briefly," her teacher stated. Tamara stuck around until the rest of the students left. "Is everything okay?"

"Yes!"

"Why have you been late for class all this week? You're usually one of the first people here."

"I will be on time from now on. Is that all you needed me

for?" Tamara asked, anxious to get to her next class.

"For now, but remember, if you ever need to talk, my door is always open," he said, sitting at his desk.

Tamara wasn't trying to fail her class, so she made a mental note to be on time from now on. The rest of the day flew by for her. As she stood outside waiting on her ride, she noticed Ed standing by a car with a bunch of his friends. They were handing something to people in exchange for money.

"Hey, Tamara, or is it Tom?" Rudy teased. Rudy was one of the girls that always made fun of Tamara in class. "Why are you staring at them? I thought you only like girls."

Rudy's friends started laughing at the joke. Tamara wished her ride would hurry up because she wanted to get away from there. A few minutes later, they all strolled off still giggling. Tamara sat on the steps and continued to watch Ed and his friends. She was amazed by all the money he held in his hand. She finally realized what he was doing to get money. It kind of intrigued her.

She waited for her ride for another forty-five minutes, before she decided to start walking. Since her mom's job was closer than walking home, she ended up going there. For it to only be 4:30 in the afternoon, the club was packed. The bouncers knew who Tamara was, so they let her right in.

"Your mom is onstage, so go straight to the dressing room and wait."

"Okay!" Tamara said, heading to the dressing room.

As she passed through the crowd, she could see her mom onstage with another female. They were rubbing baby oil all over each other. Spectators were shouting different and throwing money at them. The stage was covered with all types of bills from ones to twenties, and they continued to rain all over as the two women began to pleasure each other.

At the age of thirty-four, Akira still looked like she was only eighteen. She took really good care of her body, and it showed. Her caramel skin was nice and smooth, her perky breasts sat up nicely without a bra, and she had an ass that was as soft as a pillow. You could never tell she had two kids. Tamara was the oldest; then there was her little brother, who was only five years old. All the other strippers were jealous of Akira, and the few that weren't wanted to be part of her act.

Tamara watched on as her mom and the stripper did things she had only seen when she snuck and watched her mother's XXX videos. She had been coming to the club since she was ten. Her mom would make Tamara and lil Amin stay in the dressing room while she worked. Tamara knew almost all the people there. Some would talk about Akira for bringing her children to that type of establishment. She recently started leaving them home with her boyfriend, but Tamara didn't trust him.

"Ain't you supposed to be in the dressing room, little

girl?" one of the strippers asked, walking up on her.

Tamara turned around to see who it was. Passion stood there with her hands on her hips. She was one of the jealous ones.

"She's gonna be just like her mom, so she might as well start now," one of the other dancers chuckled, following Passion into the room.

"If you need some tips, let me know. I give good lessons," Passion said, licking her lips.

Tamara frowned her face up and sat on the couch. She wished she would have just gone home instead of coming here, even though being home with Jeff wasn't any better.

"Hurry up, y'all. We're on next," Passion said, stripping out of the lace thong set right in front of Tamara.

The other girls immediately followed by removing their outfits and changing into the ones they would be performing in. They hurried out onto the stage just as Akira and her friend finished collecting their money. Five minutes later Akira walked into the dressing room followed by a stranger. They never even noticed Tamara sitting there as Akira began performing oral sex on the man. Tamara ducked down, then hid behind the divider so they wouldn't see her.

"Ready for this?" Akira asked seductively as she leaned back onto the couch.

She spread her long legs into an expanding V, as if she were posing for a men's magazine centerfold. She parted the

lips of her juicy, tender pussy with two fingers to reward him with a beautiful view, then teasingly twirled the tip of her pearl tongue.

"Hell yeah I'm ready," the dude said. "You know every time I step in this building, I have to come get some of that."

"You got my money?" Akira asked, holding her hand out.

The dude reached into his sweatpants pocket, pulling out a huge knot of cash, then peeled off a few hundred-dollar bills. He passed the cash to Akira, who stuck it in her purse.

"Baby, you know money makes me cum, right?" she squealed as she dipped two fingers into her pussy then tasted her own juices. Her pussy was wetter than ever. "Come on and finish playing with this kitty."

Akira wore her hair slicked back in a long straight ponytail that stopped just above the split of her ass. She loved getting her hair pulled. It only made her orgasm that much stronger. Akira knew every pole and pussy popping trick in the strippers' handbook. She had been dancing since she was eighteen. It all started at NOB (Night on Broadway), and now she was that bitch at Onyx. While her body made her big money, she wanted to follow her dreams of becoming an actress, and this dude was going to help.

Rico's eyes never wavered from her hairless pussy. Her swollen glistening pair of lips called out his name, causing his swelling dick to throb in anticipation. She couldn't

believe he had this type of effect on her, since she had a man. Rico was a couple years older than her, but his dick had the stamina of an eighteen-year-old's. She was scared to leave Jeff because he would hunt her down, kill her, then probably have her kids doing the unthinkable. On the other hand, she loved fucking him. He put a hurting on her pussy, but she always wanted more.

"You see what you doing to him?" Rico asked, pointing to his erect penis.

Akira parted her lips then rolled her long tongue over the upper one. She knew that was turning him on even more.

"I could always use some more protein, but then again, it looks like he wants to expand my walls some more," Akira teased as her enticing eyes traveled all over his tall, chiseled physique.

Rico was over six feet tall, light skinned, handsome, and could eat the shit out of some pussy. No matter how much they fucked, she would still be hornier than ever. Unlike her other customers, she always came hard with him. She was addicted to his pipe, but never saw him outside of the club. He always met up with her there.

"We need to find out," he whispered.

"Tell mama you hungry," she purred softly, bringing her wet sticky finger to her lips. She slid out her tongue and proceeded to suck her own sweet pudding-like substance right off of her finger as she looked him in the eyes.

"Ummmmmm, taste like candy."

Rico nodded his head in agreement. She then reinserted her finger, pulled it out, and made her pussy blow bubbles. He enjoyed watching her do nasty tricks, especially the different ways she made herself cum. Akira knew that her being a squirter had everything to do with it.

Tamara couldn't believe her eyes as she watched her mom performing all types of acts for the man in the room.

"Mom what the hell?" was all she could say, continuing to watch. Tamara didn't know why, but she took out her cell phone and started recording them.

"Damn, baby, you stay wet." Rico was obviously enjoying the peep show too. They both were oblivious to the audience they had.

"If you want some, come get it," Akira ordered.

Rico took baby steps forward toward her. His eyes were drawn to her wet and sweet carnation-pink center as his dick aimed in her direction like a loaded Smith & Wesson, ready to cause some internal destruction. His phone went off, causing him to look down at it. It was his wife, so he ignored it. Akira watched on sheepishly, wishing she could see the look on his wife's face as she got an earful of the two of them going at it. She bet she was home pissed off right now because he didn't answer. She wanted to bust out laughing at the thought.

Rico got on his knees and crawled toward her. The desire

to have him in her mouth had sweat building on her tongue. She spread her legs as wide as they would go, and upon that notion, Rico lowered his face right into her opening. She wrapped her legs loosely around his backside and braced herself as he drove his tongue deeply inside her hole.

"Right there, baby," Akira squealed as the tip of his tongue put a gentle spanking on her clit, driving her insane.

"You like that, don't you?" he asked, nudging his nose against her as his tongue played between her slippery folds.

"Oh yesssss!" she hollered. Her eyes were practically rolling into the back of her head.

Rico slid his right middle finger inside of her while his tongue paddled through her recurring waves. Akira placed her hands on the back of his head, propped a leg over his ass, and fed her pussy to him good.

Unbeknownst to Tamara, her body started heating up. She felt her panties getting moist, and she squeezed her legs together trying to stop the leaking.

"I'm about to cum, baby!" Akira moaned.

As soon as the words left her lips, Rico stopped, flipped her over on all fours, and began devouring her from behind. He slapped her on her ass and reacted at how it bounced back against his face.

"Oooohhh shit!" Akira moaned, pulling at her left nipple ring, loving the pain it brought.

"This what you wanted, huh?"

"Yessss, baby, punish this pussy!" she shouted. "Don't you cheat me out of my fucking nut."

Tamara was so turned on, that she didn't care anymore as her fluids soaked her panties. She even moaned a bit, listening to her mother getting her pussy eaten from behind. Akira could tell by how hard Rico's dick felt against her ass that he was on the brink of explosion. He blindly reached in his pocket and grabbed the last magnum condom out of the pack.

He slipped it on quickly, all the while continuing his feast, forcing her to reach another climax so big that she squirted all over his face. He lifted his face from her crotch and let his tongue skinny dip along the riverbanks of her asshole.

"I'ma teach you to stop nutting until I say when—" Rico stopped in mid-sentence when he saw someone peeking from around the divider. He was hard as a brick and about one second from making his grand entrance inside of her before the abrupt interruption. "I thought you said no one was in here?"

"There's not! I locked the door," she replied, looking toward the dressing room door.

"Who that behind the divider then?"

Tamara was scared that she had been caught spying on her mom. She tried to find somewhere else to hide but couldn't. Akira walked over, then pulled the divider back.

"What are you doing here? You're supposed to be home with Jeff," she said, wrapping the robe over her naked body.

"He never came, so I came here to wait for you," Tamara replied.

"Why didn't you call?"

"I tried, but neither of you answered the phone."

"That's your daughter?" Rico asked, thinking she was a dude the way she dressed.

"Yes!"

"I have to get out of here, but we need to finish this at my place tonight."

"You know I only do that here," she whispered so Tamara couldn't hear them.

"Well, since we were interrupted, you need to make an exception. Here, get her some real clothes so no one gets her confused with being someone else," he said, peeling off three more hundred-dollar bills, and tossing them to Akira. He walked toward the door. "Call me when you're ready."

Rico walked out the door before she could respond. Tamara didn't know what was about to happen to her right now. She braced herself for the repercussions.

"You didn't see anything that happened here, understand?"

"Yes," Tamara said, wondering why her mom didn't snap out.

Akira got dressed, then counted all the money that she

made off of Rico. She knew it came at a price though, and that price was meeting up with him later. This was going to be the first time she broke her rule, but not the last.

TWO

"Where's your momma at?" Jeff asked Tamara.

"She had to go back to work," she replied, giving her lil brother his food. "Why didn't you pick me up from school?"

"I was busy, and don't be questioning my whereabouts. I go where I want, when I want. You just worry about your brother and stay in your lane."

Tamara didn't respond; she just ate her food. Every time she looked at Jeff reminded her why she hated him so much. She couldn't understand why her mother stayed with him. He would put his hands on her whenever she didn't do as he pleased. There were plenty of nights she would wake up to her mom hollering at him, or the other way around. Tamara said she wouldn't ever let a man put his hands on her. No woman deserved to be treated like shit.

After cleaning the kitchen and putting her brother to bed, Tamara decided to catch up on the new *Claws* series, when Jeff came downstairs in his boxers. He always walked around the house half naked, and didn't care who was around.

"Go to the store and grab me two green games," he demanded, then passed her a ten-dollar bill.

Tamara was about to protest, but changed her mind. Besides, she wanted to get away from him anyway, even if it was only for a few minutes. As she walked down the street,

she noticed a group of boys standing on the corner. One of them just happened to be Ed, and once again he had a knot of cash in his hands. They were laughing and joking as two fiends took turns letting the other boys punch them in the face. They were betting each other to see who could knock the fiends out with one punch. Ed was waving the money in their faces, encouraging them to take it.

"Whoever is still standing after this wins the hundred dollars," Ed shouted. He sat the money on the ground, then prepared for his turn. His homies had their cell phones out recording the show so they could laugh at it later.

Tamara stood there for a minute, watching Ed as he punched the first fiend. The fiend went straight down and didn't move. The second fiend took the punch like a pro. His nose was leaking, but he didn't go down. Ed gave the fiend some baggies instead of the cash, and he ran off to smoke it with his buddy. When he looked up, Tamara was staring at him. She quickly turned away then walked into the store. She grabbed a few things to snack on, then placed them on the counter.

"Let me get two green games," she said to the clerk.

"I didn't know you smoked," someone said from behind.

Tamara turned around to see Ed standing behind her. "I don't!" she said, shaking her head letting him know that she didn't, then passed the money to the clerk. She could see him holding a twenty-dollar bill in his hand. He slid it into her pocket. "What's that for?"

"That's for the money you just spent. You're in my class, right?"

"Yeah, and here's your money back," she said, pulling it out of her pocket and holding it out to him.

"If you don't mind me asking, why do you dress like that?" Ed said.

"None of your business. Now if you'll excuse me, I have to get home," Tamara replied, sat the money in front of him, then started for the door. Ed ran up behind her and secretly slid the money back in her pocket.

"Wait, I have a question for you." Tamara stopped and turned around. "Can you tutor me? I really need help passing this class so I can get out of school this year. It's important to me."

"Why me?" she asked curiously.

"Because you seem like you're very smart. I will pay you whatever you want. Money ain't shit to me."

"Um, I'll let you know," she said, walking down the street with a smile on her face. She was ecstatic that he even knew who she was.

"See you in class!" he shouted.

When she returned home, Jeff was sitting on the steps smoking a cigarette. He had on a pair of shorts and a wifebeater.

"Damn, what took you so long?"

Tamara ignored his question, gave him the Dutches, and then rushed up to her room. She couldn't stop blushing about

the brief conversation her and Ed had. She had fantasized about him twice already, and even though she was a virgin, the dreams. were very hot and steamy. Her pussy was wet just thinking about him. She took a shower, then went to bed hoping she had another wet dream.

~ ~ ~

It was four in the morning when Tamara woke up to a strange noise. She got out of bed and crept out of the room to see what was going on. As she passed by the bathroom, she heard a soft grunt coming from inside. The door was cracked, so she peeped inside. Jeff was sitting on the toilet playing with himself. Tamara frowned up her face but stood there watching him. He had his eyes closed, so he didn't even know he was being watched.

"Ughh," Jeff blurted out as he jumped up and shot his load inside the toilet.

Tamara didn't know why, but watching other people pleasure themselves as well as others was beginning to have a toll on her. She found herself getting turned on each time she saw it. Even though she didn't like Jeff, the sight of his massive cock had her wet once again. When she heard the front door shut, she ran back to her room.

Her mom had just come home from the club. Tamara jumped back in bed, acting like she was asleep. She didn't know if her mom was still mad about what she witnessed in

the dressing room earlier or not, but she wasn't taking any chances. If she knew she was watching her boyfriend pleasing himself, she definitely would snap out. The door opened, and Akira walked in.

"Tamara, wake up," she whispered. "Tamara!"

"Hmmmm," Tamara replied, acting like she just woke up.

"I need to talk to you about earlier."

"Oh boy, I knew it," she said under her breath. She prepared for the lecture, but to her surprise, it never came. Akira talked calmly to her.

"What you seen tonight is part of how I make the money that takes care of you and your brother and puts food on the table every night. I'm not proud of the things I've done, but I sure as hell don't regret any of it. God has blessed me with this beautiful body, and I intend to use it until I can't use it any longer. Have you ever taken the time to look at yourself in the mirror?"

"I always do, Mom," Tamara replied, wondering what she was getting at.

"Tamara, you are a beautiful young lady. Your body has gone through different changes, and you should be proud of it. I even bought you clothes that you won't even wear. Are you ashamed of your curves?"

"No, I just don't want people staring at me when I walk down the street. They're always making smart comments as it is."

"That's because you only wear sweatpants and other baggy clothes. Try dressing like a girl. I only have one son and one daughter, so act like it."

"I'm fine with how I dress," Tamara said confidently.

"Fuck that. You are old enough to start helping with the bills around here, and that's exactly what you're going to do," Akira snapped. "So get your head on straight because shit is about to change around here."

"Jeff don't work," Tamara stated. She wondered why her mother was acting like that. "Did I do something wrong?"

"No, I just want you to wise up and understand what's going on out here in these streets. You have to use what you got, to get what you want. As long as you have that precious gem between your legs, you should never be broke," she stated blankly. "And don't worry, his ass gonna do something too, or kick rocks. I have to be somewhere right now. We'll finish this conversation when you get home from school later on. Drop your brother off at the daycare, because his lazy-ass father won't do it."

When Akira left the room, Tamara realized just what her mother was trying to say. She lay back down and tried to think of a way to help out.

THREE

Later that day when Akira walked into her house, the pungent fish odor caused her nose to turn up. She figured Jeff had forgotten to take the trash out before he left to meet up with his friends.

"God, that motherfucker is good for nothing," she cursed under her breath, realizing she had to do everything herself.

She located the bottle of Febreze air freshener, aired the place out, then hurried to take out the garbage. When she returned, she checked the time before rushing to the bathroom to shower after spending the last few hours with the dude from the club. She had at least three hours to freshen up and take a nap before she had to be back at work. Today was two-dollar Tuesday, and if you wanted to make a lot of money, you had to come in early. She was supposed to be the headliner tonight.

Dripping wet, Akira grabbed a towel from the closet and dried off. She quickly dressed in a pair of white, sheer, booty-strangling boy shorts, and a matching sheer wifebeater. She lay across her king-sized bed and dozed right off. Those couple of hours flew past, and she hopped up, rushed to the bathroom to brush her teeth, then unwrapped her hair.

She slipped on some sandals and grabbed her traveling

case, which held her outfits for tonight's show. Also inside was a change of clothes, several pairs of G-strings, toiletries, and makeup. Akira was going to kill the stage tonight like it was her last performance. After loading her bag in the backseat, she called Jeff to make sure he was going pick up the kids.

"Yo, what's up?" he answered on the third ring.

"Don't forget to pick up your son and Tamara today."

"I'll get my son, but your daughter can chill with you. She's too fucking hardheaded, and I don't have time for that," he replied.

"She can take care of herself," Akira said. "Just drive her home, asshole." She hung up on him.

A half an hour later, Akira entered through the door of the infamous Onyx. Judging by the parking lot, it was a full house already. The energy was high, the music was bumping, and Akira would bet that there were at least two hundred rock-hard dicks waiting to get close and personal with her. Everyone knew she was going to turn up in that joint as soon as they saw her.

Akira always made the most money and had the most customers return, and all the other strippers respected her hustle, because she was one of the oldest there. She never used the private rooms for her platinum customers. She would use the dressing room so they could have fun, and no one disturbed her for the thirty minutes she needed. In fact,

those that weren't getting it like she was sat back and took notes.

She spoke to a few of the girls as she passed by them giving lap dances to the horny men. She always made a point to be extra nice to the waitresses. They were like her agents in a way. They informed her when there were goldmines on the premises, and led her right to them. Melissa, also known as Chocolate Butter, was a white girl trapped in a black girl's body. Men loved her because she was built like a stallion and was very pretty. In the exotic industry, that's all it took for you to be successful.

"Hey, Moét!" Melissa said as Akira walked up. "Girl, you're going to make some money up in this joint tonight. Most of the men here have been asking for you."

"Already? That's definitely what I wanted to hear. How'd you do so far?"

"Not so good. But, hey, the day is still young, and we still have tonight."

Akira nodded, knowing that was wishful thinking because once she hit the stage, she was going to suck the blood out of every dick in there while draining their pockets. So there wouldn't be any leftovers. It took no time for her to transform into her alter ego. When she finished, she double-checked herself in the mirror, then anxiously headed out to the floor.

"Now, fellas, I got something real wet and nasty in store

for you tonight," Akira heard the DJ announce.

She peeked from behind the curtain to see that the club was jam-packed all the way from the bar to the main stage. There wasn't an empty seat in sight, and the men, and women that looked like men, began clapping and yelling for him to bring on the show.

"They're out there for you," Passion said, standing next to Akira.

"You already know what time it is. I know it's two-dollar Tuesday, but this fine hot piece of ass is what I call a double shot!" The crowd roared in excitement as they waved and flashed the money in their hands. "Onyx, get your money together so we can pay some bills in this bitch! Now show some love for my girl, Moét."

Her theme music started to play, and she came from behind the curtain donning a super-sexy sheer leopard print bra and skirt, trimmed with black fur. Her matching garter straps and seven-inch stilettos only added to the wicked fantasy she hoped would fulfill her regulars and prospective regulars tonight. She swayed her hips to the song's prelude.

Her oiled skin was dusted in a shimmering gold glitter, and her sixteen-inch hair weave draped past her shoulders and down her back. She surveyed the club, making eye contact with every eye in the room, as she moved her body to the beat beginning to fuse in. She began mouthing her heavily glossed lips to the lyrics of Miguel and Kendrick

Lamar's "How Many Drinks" as she danced, translating the words sexually: "Frustration, watching you dance. Hesitation, to get in your pants. Come closer, so I can touch. One question, am I moving to fast?"

Akira slowly began to shed her bra. As she did so, money began to fly from every direction of the room. She moved her body in a sexy rhythm as she slid out her long tongue. She squeezed her oiled luscious breasts together and flicked the leopard spiked ball across both of her pierced nipples. The crowd went wild!

"How many drinks would it take you to be with me? Yeah, you look good, and I got money and I don't wanna waste your time. Back of my mind, I'm hoping you would say two or three, you look good, we came to party, but I don't wanna waste my time."

She could feel all eyes on her, and that was enough to get her pussy wet and leaking with excitement. She teasingly danced out of her skirt, then slid to the floor. Akira crawled across the stage, collecting money with her mouth and breasts. When she found her biggest tipper, she did her signature move.

She scooted to the edge of the stage, spread her legs wide-open in a V shape, and made her pussy blow bubbles. He started popping bands and began dealing out a full stack. The sight of the money made her cum so hard, that her juices squirted out into the crowd. Akira counted at least a grand,

and was positive that it was more. She couldn't see his face due to the darkness of the club, but she could see the green flying out of his hands.

"That's right, y'all, let those bills fly," the DJ yelled over the mic.

She lay all the way back then jiggled her legs and thighs in the air, making her ass clap like crazy. Moét stretched her legs into an upside down split and motioned for the dude spending the money to come closer. She grabbed one of the bills he'd just thrown at her, laid it across her pussy, and seconds later, the bill went twirling in the air, landing right on her stomach. She did it a second time for the people who couldn't believe it the first time.

The dude leaned in to place his face closer between her thighs. He ran his long fingers across her pubic area, and she could feel his fingers tracing her tattoo. Without a break in her performance, she started to grind on his entire arm like it was a foot-long dick. Money continued to fly from every direction, but the dude who was still palming her pussy had all of her attention. When the song ended, Akira leaned forward in his ear.

"We can go in the back if you want a real private dance."

"I knew the second I walked in this motherfucker that that was you up on that stage," he said, removing his glasses.

"Oh shit, is that you, Gene?" Akira uttered, barely able to catch her breath.

"Get your stuff and let's blow this joint."

Akira quickly hopped up, collected all her money, and rushed offstage. She couldn't believe her past had come back to visit her. Gene was Tamara's biological father. He had been locked up for a shooting, and they had given him twenty-five years in prison. Now he was back home in less than fifteen. She hoped like hell he didn't plan on staying or trying to see his daughter, who he claimed wasn't his.

FOUR

Since Akira was out with who knows who, Jeff decided to hook up with one of the girls at the club who had been trying to give him some pussy. He was tired of beating his dick every night, and snuck over to where Passion, whose real name was Kayla, lived. They had sex all night until falling asleep in each other's arms. Kayla knew who he was messing with, but didn't care. In all actuality, she was jealous of Akira.

The sound of the door opening and closing woke Jeff up. He realized he wasn't home and jumped up. He cursed under his breath as he threw his boxers and jeans on as fast as he could. A million things ran through his mind as he dressed. One of them was if she would go running her mouth to Akira. Although he cheated on her, he still cared because she was the mother of his child.

Kayla was more like the chick you call when you want a quick shot of pussy. She would be there in a heartbeat for that money. When she informed him of what Akira was doing behind closed doors at the club, his pride felt like it had been walked on, his feelings pissed on, and his heart shitted on, all by a woman—a woman he was gonna make his wife one day. Those thoughts went out the door though when he found out that she was drinking other men's cum.

Now all he expected from women was pussy and conversation. It was all he would allow any woman to give him generously.

He headed into the living room and found the front door wide open. He could faintly hear Kayla arguing with someone outside as their voices carried into her second-floor apartment. Jeff hurried down the stairs and trudged toward the commotion brewing in the parking lot, unsure as to what was going on.

"I said don't touch me!"

"Bitch, who the fuck you think you're talking to? I want my fucking money, and I'm not leaving here until I get it. One way or the other, you're gonna give me what I came for."

"I told you I don't have it right now," Kayla shouted.

"Well I'll just take that then," he said, pointing to her car. "Give me the fucking keys."

"Hey, hey, hey. What's going on?" Jeff asked. His eyes darted from a hysterical Kayla to the tall skinny dude dressed in jeans and a tight T-shirt.

"This bitch owes me money, and I want my shit."

"Yo, watch your mouth, first and foremost," Jeff stated, trying to flex his muscles a bit. He usually didn't get involve with domestic shit, but he was trying to earn some cool points with Kayla. "How much do she owe you?"

"She owes me fifteen hundred dollars. Why? Who the

fuck is you?" he asked, not backing down.

"Listen, my man, I just asked you a question. It ain't that deep. She said she don't have it, so you're gonna have to wait, but you're not gonna take her car."

The dude got too close to Jeff, trying to size him up. Before he knew what was happening, Jeff was hitting him with a barrage of punches. He hit the ground hard, banging his head on the ground. Jeff started kicking him in the face, trying to knock his teeth out.

"The cops coming," Kayla yelled to Jeff.

"Now get the fuck out of here, and when she gets your money, she'll pay you."

He headed back inside with Kayla on his heels. Once back in the apartment, Jeff checked his fist, making sure there wasn't any blood on him.

"Thank you so much for that," Kayla said, giving him a hug.

"What you owe him that much money for?"

"It's a long story," she replied.

"Well I'm gonna take a quick shower, and then you can tell me why I just stomped some dude out in front of your crib," Jeff replied, heading into the bathroom.

Once she heard the shower water running, Kayla grabbed her cell phone and made a quick call to someone. She talked briefly with the person on the other end, then ended the call. She smiled to herself as she headed back into the bedroom.

When she opened the drawer, there was a stack of money inside.

"I'm not giving you shit, pussy, and if you come back, I have something for you," she said, reaching back in the drawer under her panties and pulling out her .25 automatic. She checked it momentarily, then placed it back in the drawer. She walked over and lay across the bed, waiting for Jeff to finish.

~ ~ ~

Ten minutes later, Jeff exited the bathroom wearing only a towel. He walked over and sat on the edge of the bed. Kayla was lying there like she was asleep when he tapped her on the shoulder.

"Yo, tell me what that was all about."

Just as she sat up to say something, there was a knock at the door. Jeff looked at her wondering if dude had come back with a gun this time wanting more.

"Let me get that," Kayla said, getting off the bed. She sensed the caution on his face and eased the tension. "It's for me, don't worry."

She went to answer the door, and when she returned, she wasn't alone. Standing in the doorway with her was some white girl. She was skinny, but her body was tight with pale skin.

"This is my friend Sheila, and we wanted to thank you for what you did earlier," Kayla said, then turned to Sheila and started kissing her.

Kayla started untying her halter top. Sheila responded by placing her hands on Kayla's ass, then pulling off her shorts. The top came off and Jeff was staring directly at Sheila's breasts. They were petite compared to Kayla's gorgeous melons, but high, round, and perfectly shaped. The nipples hardened as Kayla placed her mouth on each one of them. Jeff's dick immediately started rising to the occasion, watching in fascination.

Kayla raised her head and they began kissing again, their mouths fusing together and their tongues working. Sheila's fingers were working overtime at her crotch, causing Kayla to squirm and pant. She broke the kiss, placing her hands over Sheila's breasts.

"You like it dirty, huh?"

Sheila had a hand between Kayla's legs, with two fingers inside her pussy, and one diddling her clit, while the other hand rubbed her ass. As Jeff watched, Sheila found Kayla's anus with her forefinger and began to slide it inside. Kayla gasped, her body jerking uncontrollably and her hands tightened on Sheila's breasts.

"Yes," she moaned. "Yes, I do. You know I do, you sweet little bitch."

"Then let's do it," Sheila said hoarsely. "I'm gonna fuck

you till you scream, and your friend will watch it all."

Their words were getting Jeff excited, as were their actions. As they lay on the bed together, Jeff slowly removed the towel, exposing his throbbing dick for all to see. Sheila helped Kayla out of her shirt while she removed her shorts. Jeff was fascinated by how beautiful Sheila's pussy looked. It was much juicier than Kayla's.

Both naked now, the women attacked each other with their hands and mouths, licking, sucking, and stroking every inch of each other's body. Jeff couldn't take his eyes off of the two contrasting bodies, one so dark and voluptuously curved, and the other pale, and slender, but sensuous and supple. Their bodies twisted, squirmed, and rolled until they were positioned crotch to crotch, with their heads pointing in different directions. Their legs forking each other's body as they rubbed their pussies together.

Loud moaning and gasping sounds came from both of them as they continued to fool around on the bed, with Jeff watching the action. Jeff started to massage his dick because he couldn't contain himself. Sheila looked at him with slightly glazed eyes, grinning at him.

"You like this, huh?" Sheila grunted. "You like the way I'm fucking your friend?"

"Fuck me, baby," Kayla said, gasping out the words. "Ohh Christ . . . yes . . . fuck . . . yessss, I'm about to cum."

Her body started jerking so hard that her huge breasts

shuddered and bounced with each spasm. Minutes later, Sheila followed suit and climaxed also.

After they both caught their breath, Sheila began eating Kayla's pussy again, trying to make her have another orgasm. She turned toward Jeff and licked her lips.

"Come on, baby," Sheila panted at Jeff. "Come fuck this pussy now."

"Yes, you better fuck her brains out," Kayla moaned, out of breath.

Jeff couldn't resist the temptation any longer, even if he wanted to. The show was over, and now it was time to get in on the action. He got up and crouched down behind Sheila. He reached around and put his hands on her breasts. Her hip movements slowed, allowing him to position his dick at the opening of her pussy. He pushed in slowly, causing her to gasp softly and stiffen up for a moment. Then she began moving faster to meet his thrust. Her pussy was tight and hot around his aching dick.

As he plunged repeatedly into her body, the force of his thrust added to the force of hers as she continued eating Kayla's pussy. She was going crazy, babbling, bucking, and jerking. Jeff knew he wouldn't be able to hold out much longer, the way Sheila's pussy was milking and tugging at his dick.

"Oh shit, I'm about to cum," he mumbled.

He didn't know who came first, but he thought it was

Sheila. Even though she cried out and he could feel her pussy twitching and spasming as she climaxed, her orgasm was still kind of gentle compared to Kayla's. Her screams were deafening, and the convulsions of her body nearly threw the two of them off her. Jeff shot his full load into Sheila, not even thinking about if she was on the pill or not.

They all collapsed on the bed, and Jeff tried to fall asleep. The next thing he knew, Kayla was leaning over him, kissing him gently. She worked her way down his body until she reached his limp dick. She placed it into her mouth, and started sucking on it. He didn't stay limp for long as her tongue ring did its job. Sheila was lying alongside, watching with a smile on her face, while she sucked him to another climax.

"I hope it was as good for you as it was for me," Sheila said, putting her clothes back on and heading for the door.

"Damn, I'm beat," Jeff replied.

"Good! No man can handle this white chocolate."

"We have to do that again," Kayla said, walking Sheila out and then giving her a passionate kiss on the lips.

"For sure! Just call me," Sheila replied, walking next door to her apartment.

When Kayla came back inside, Jeff was lying there trying to get himself together before he headed back home. The conversation they were supposed to have was now nonexistent. They had fucked and sucked him so good that

he had forgotten all about it. Kayla smiled to herself, because that's exactly what she was trying to do, and it worked. She didn't need him all up in her business even though he already beat the shit out of the dude. That was a problem she would handle by herself real soon.

FIVE

Akira lay there for a minute. Her head was throbbing and spinning. She definitely had a hangover. She wondered if it was even possible to get carpal tunnel in the neck; if so, she had that too from sucking so much dick last night. She'd never felt so damn bad in her life.

She eased up, careful not to wake Gene up. As she scanned the room, she saw liquor bottles, cigarillos, and a bag of weed sitting on the stand below the wall-mounted flat-screen. It smelled like a concoction of sweaty butt-naked sex, weed, and alcohol, with a hint of her sweet perfume. She began to recall most of what took place last night, causing her throbbing head to pound even more. Akira slowly climbed out of bed, feeling so lightheaded she thought she was going to faint.

Still in only her birthday suit, she walked around the king-size bed in search of her heels. She eased into them and staggered toward the bathroom, grabbing her phone in the process. The liquor hadn't quite worn off, so every step was a balancing act. She needed to call and check up on her kids.

"Hello," a groggy voice answered.

"Tamara, is you up getting ready for school?"

"Yes!" she lied.

"Okay, make sure you get your brother ready for the daycare also."

"I know, Mom. I do it every morning," she replied, irritated.

"I'm sending an Uber to pick y'all up in a half hour," she said, looking at the time. "If you need money, you know where to find it." She hung up and sat on the toilet to piss.

Spending time with Gene last night felt like old times. Instead of taking her to a hotel, he wanted to crash at her spot for the night. She refused to show him where she lived, especially since she was living with Jeff. There was no way in hell that was going down. She didn't know what new situation he had going on, and she wasn't about to jeopardize her or her kids' lives any more than she already had.

She figured the less they both knew about each other, the better. After using the bathroom, she walked over to the sink, looking in the mirror. It wasn't a pretty sight. She had bags under her eyes, no makeup, and her hair was all over the place. She began fixing the pieces of hair that were out of place because even after oversleeping for most of the morning, a bitch like her had to look good. She washed up and then put on some more makeup and lipstick.

"Ummm . . ." Gene moaned.

Akira came out of the bathroom and walked over to get a glass of water. When she turned around, he was staring at her.

"What?" she said, looking at him.

"I see somebody getting ready for another round," Gene said as he got up from the bed and headed over to her.

The first thing she pointed to was the huge hickey on the left side of her neck. He just smirked at her like it was nothing.

"You're just getting reacquainted with this and already trying to mark your territory?"

"Damn right! I'm about to mark it again," Gene said, pointing to his hard-on. He slapped her on the ass, then headed for the bathroom. After he was done, he walked back over to her and started kissing her.

He kissed her as if they had never left each other. It felt like they were picking up right where they'd left off, but in the back of Akira's mind, she knew differently. A lot had changed over the last fifteen years, and although Gene was Tamara's father, they both belonged to two entirely different worlds now. She had kind of missed him, and yearned for his touch. Now that he was here, in the flesh, giving her body what it wanted and had been missing, she didn't know what else to do other than fuck him in memory of lost time. She could feel her juices flowing as Gene slipped his hands between her legs to wake up her kitty.

"Ummm . . . yes . . . oh shit," she moaned. Her round swollen nipples poked at his chest. "Damn, that feels so good, baby. You know how to tame this pussy."

Gene was hovering at six feet. He had a medium build and wide chest, with pure solid muscles in his arms. He still had the belly that she used to tease him about. The braids that he used to rock were now replaced by a low cut, with

waves flowing like the sea. He still had his beard, only it was longer now because he had become Muslim while incarcerated. His arms were both covered with sleeve tattoos. The one she admired the most was his neck tattoo with her name on it. He'd gotten it the same time she'd gotten hers.

All and all, Gene was still that pretty boy from the hood that she fell in love with when she was seventeen. He picked her up and sat her on the edge of the counter. As he gradually spread her legs, he kissed and tongued both of her thighs, then worked his way to the middle. Akira panted and moaned in satisfaction as her pussy began to melt from his touch. Her nipples hardened as she braced herself for another Red Roof Inn adventure. She'd been there so many times that she knew the night crew by name.

Her head fell back against the wall, and that cold touch against her shoulders and back sent a surge of energy below. Her hands were at either side, giving him the leverage he needed to eat her pussy properly.

"Now this is how I like my breakfast," Gene said, driving his tongue in and out of her.

Akira purred like a kitten as he gave her some serious head. She was thinking he hadn't lost his touch one bit as she watched his head bobble with every stroke. She extended her legs further until her ankles were hooked over her shoulders. The pointy heel of her stilettos jabbed the mirror with every tongue thrust. It felt so good, and she couldn't help how wet

she was for him. If she never told him she missed it, he knew now.

"Get that shit!" Akira egged him on as he swallowed her pussy whole. She could feel her nut getting ready to crack. She was right there and could see the finish line approaching with a couple more licks.

It was like Gene knew it too, because right then he changed up. He must not have been ready for her to shoot her load. He pushed her knees toward her chest as if she were getting ready to give birth, then slowly prepared to lay his pipe down sideways.

"Oh yessss!" Akira gasped as he entered her. Her entire body stiffened at first, and she tried to clench something, but there was nothing next to her to grab. "Oh my God!" she panted as the back of her head occasionally bounced against the wall.

"Whose pussy is this?" Gene asked.

"It's yours! Do what you want to it."

He gripped her hips and gave it to her full throttle. Akira's breasts flopped around as he pounded into her. Gene slapped her on the ass, remembering how she liked it. His pace quickened as he drove farther into her love box. He tightened his grip around her waist and hit every single corner of her pussy. When he managed to find her G-spot, Akira began screaming in pure ecstasy. As if that was all the encouragement he needed, Gene raised her legs above her head and gave her one final swerve.

"Arrggghhh!" Gene grunted. His face contorted as he exploded so deeply inside of Akira that her body jerked. She had arrived with him.

"Oh shiitttt," she screamed, releasing her fluids.

A smile swept across Gene's face as he leaned in to kiss her. He slowly slid out of her, releasing both of their milky liquids along the way. Akira sat up.

"Let's hit the shower," Gene said.

"You go ahead. I'll take mine at home. I know Tamara and DJ is probably worried sick about me, so I better roll out."

"You have another kid?" he questioned.

"Yes, I have a son, and I stay with his father," Akira replied. "That's the reason we couldn't go back to my place last night. It just wouldn't have been right to him."

"Well, you have to tell that nigga that he have to go, now that I'm back in the picture." Gene didn't crack a smile.

"Yeah, well that's not gonna happen."

"What you mean?"

"Exactly what I said. You just can't come back in the picture like everything is all peaches and cream now. A lot has changed in fifteen years, Gene," Akira snapped.

"I tried reaching out to you, Akira. I called your mom, your cousin, everybody that fucking knew you, and they told me you moved away somewhere because you had a new job."

"I did, but that doesn't change the fact that you left me

hanging out there. I thought you were dead." She paused, feeling tears building up in her eyes. "I didn't know what happened to you. First, I'm hearing you owed some dangerous people some money and skipped town. Then the next I'm hearing is they caught you and killed you. I didn't know what the fuck to believe. I had to bounce because I thought me and my daughter's life was in danger too!"

"Listen, that shit was mostly true. I did have to leave because niggas was after me, and when a couple of them caught up to me, I shot them. The cops didn't buy my story, and I ended up getting all that time. I never said anything to you because I didn't want to put you and Tamara in danger."

"But you still left me though," Akira said. "How do I know that they're not still looking for you?"

"If they were, they could have got at me in prison," he lied.

Truth was, he had taken protective custody so they didn't kill him. When he was released, he jumped on a plane to Philly, hoping to get away. When he went out to the strip club, he didn't expect to see Akira there. That was just fate.

"I had no money, no car, no clothes or food. My family wouldn't fuck with me 'cause I chose you over them. You took all that money and stepped, leaving me with nothing. I came here to start a new life, and that's what I did."

"I had no idea I would end up in prison, or else I would have left the money with you."

"So that money you was throwing around in the club last

night is the money you stole from those peoples?" she asked curiously.

When he didn't respond, that only confirmed what she was already thinking. There was no doubt in her mind that they were a done deal. It wasn't because she didn't still love him. It was because she didn't trust him and didn't want to put her kids in danger. She knew those people were still going to come after him. That was a lot of money he stole.

"That's what I figured," she said, answering for him. "This ain't for me anymore. I will not let my kids be harmed over some nigga."

"That money I took is what put you halfway through school, so don't forget that." She cut her eyes up at him, then fell silent. "Listen, Akira, I understand that you done found a new life out here, but I still love you. Always have, and always will."

"You're not listening to me. I have a new family now. I never stopped loving you either, but I moved on when you left me, and there's no turning back."

"You call shaking your ass in some strip club moving on?" He chuckled.

"You know what," Akira said, climbing down from the counter, "it was good seeing you again, but I gotta bounce."

"Wait a minute!" Gene said, grabbing her by the elbow. "You ain't going no fucking where! We still talking." Akira tried pulling her arm away, but Gene's grip was too tight.

"Owww, you're hurting me!" she said, trying her best to

wiggle her arm away from him.

He finally let her go, and she hurried over to the chair to throw on her clothes. She didn't care about anything else except for getting the hell out of there fast as she could. She grabbed her keys off the end table and jetted for the door.

"Akira!" Gene called after her as she hurried down the hall, passing the cleaning lady who had just come out of one of the rooms.

"Ma'am, I think he's trying to get your attention," the lady called out to her, but she kept on walking until she reached the stairs. She rushed down and through the lobby pissed, and from the stares she was receiving, everyone knew it.

Akira jumped into her car and sped out of the parking garage. She didn't look in her rearview until she was back on the highway. The sight of the Red Roof Inn became smaller and smaller by the second. As for Gene, he was another long-lost memory, and that's exactly where she planned on keeping him.

SIX

"Ahhhhh, that bitch thinks she's gonna play me?" Rajon said, throwing his glass at the wall. "I'm gonna show her and that nigga that snuck me. Load the fuck up! We gonna make an example out of somebody tonight."

He was pissed that Kayla acted like she didn't owe him money for the dope she copped off of him. Usually, she would pay him at the end of the week for the work, but she was almost three weeks late. To him, that was a sign of weakness, and if people thought he was weak, they would try to run all over him. That was something he couldn't tolerate.

"Let's go start some ruckus," Ray said, cocking the gun he held in his hand.

"No doubt," Rajon replied as they headed out.

Ray knew one of the niggas that was handling shit for Kayla. He had called and told him his cousin wanted to meet up with him. Since he couldn't go, he sent his mans. He pulled up in a black tinted-out Cherokee.

"You want me to handle it?" Ray asked.

"No! You wait here. I got this. This bitch needs to know that any of her peoples, including her, can be touched," Rajon said, exiting the car.

He walked over and hopped in the passenger's seat. The

driver pulled off and cruised down the one-way street at a moderate speed. The Hemi engine roared even with the gas pedal barely being tapped. Ray followed about five cars behind so he wasn't noticed.

"Just got this new batch in this morning," the driver said with excitement. "It's still fresh. This is some fire, bro." He tapped the bag that was sitting on his lap.

"My baby, Kayla, said she had some good shit out here with y'all," Rajon said casually as he peeked in the mirror to his right. He quickly scanned the entire area, and once the cars behind him were gone, he pulled the .40 cal from his waistband. He pointed and placed it just inches away from the dude's head. "Pull this fucking car over, and don't try anything."

The driver looked over with great surprise, and as a natural reflex he backhanded the gun out of his face. The Cherokee swerved as the driver tried to gain control of it. The backhand caused Rajon to lose his firm grip. As he attempt to regain his grip, the driver punched him smooth on the chin. The blow caught him totally off guard. It took him seconds before he could even react. Rajon squeezed the trigger with rage.

Bloca!

The gunshot echoed loudly, temporarily deafening both of them. All they both could hear was continuous ringing in their ears. The pungent smell of gunpowder filled the truck.

The film from the gun smoke fogged the windows, making it difficult to see out of them. The hot slug penetrated the driver's shoulder. The metal shot through his nerves like a bolt of electricity, causing him to lose total control of the wheel. The Jeep swerved to the right and hopped onto the sidewalk before slamming into the gate that surrounded an abandoned house.

When the Jeep came to a stop, the driver forced the door open and fled the vehicle clumsily, in an attempt to get away. Rajon sat there dizzy from the crash. As he shook away the wooziness, he saw the driver making a stumbling getaway. Rajon's focal point was the shopping bag that he held tightly in his hand.

Rajon hopped out of the Jeep and chased behind him, both of them so dizzy, they were stumbling. The dude's feet crossed and he tumbled over. Before he could land, Rajon was already standing over the top of him, with his gun aimed at the back of his head.

Bloca!

The dude's neck snapped forward from the impact, causing his face to bang against the concrete, full contact. Rajon dumped two more shots into the back of his skull just in case. He released the shopping bag from his grasp, and it fell next to his lifeless body. Rajon picked up the bag, then dashed across the street, just as Ray pulled up. He had been watching the whole time, ready to intervene if needed.

"Let's bounce," he told Ray as he jumped in, closing the door behind him.

They sped down the block in the opposite direction, racing through traffic. Once they were a safe distance away from the scene, Ray slowed down until they were cruising with the regular traffic.

"How much is it?" Ray asked, watching him count the contents.

"It's a hundred bundles of dope and two pounds of marijuana."

"Damn, why was he carrying all that around?"

"Don't know and don't care. Now we have her shit. No wonder she hasn't been copping from me," he said, closing the bag. "She was getting it from somewhere else. She's a sorry-ass bitch. I can't wait to catch her and that nigga she was with. This should make up for what she owes, plus some."

"I'm with you, Cousin," Ray replied.

"No, I need you to take care of that," Rajon said, pointing to the bag. "We'll break that shit right down the middle when you're done."

"I got you, Cuz! Say no more," Ray shouted, excited that his cousin was showing so much love. He wasn't expecting that much, but he wasn't going to object either.

After getting dropped off at his ride, Rajon jumped into his wheel and headed home, finally at peace with the

decision he made. He had wished it would have been Kayla or the nigga she was with, but fuck it.

~ ~ ~

"So are you going to tutor me or not?" Ed asked Tamara when he sat at his desk.

"I, I'm not sure yet," she replied, turning around in her seat.

"Why are you so shy to talk to me? Once you get to know me, I'm a good person."

"I'm not shy, and yes, I will tutor you," she said, giving in to him being so persistent.

"Great! When can we start?" Ed whispered.

"Umm, meet me in the library today at lunchtime."

"I'll be there," he replied, sitting back in his seat. Tamara was smiling from ear to ear for the rest of the class and couldn't wait till lunch.

~ ~ ~

Tamara sat in the library waiting for Ed to show up for his tutoring session. While waiting, she decided to read a book called *Supreme & Justice*, by Ernest Morris. She checked the time on her cell phone and noticed that lunch was almost over. Just as she was about to leave, Ed came

strolling in counting a handful of money. Tamara was once again impressed at how he always walked around with a pocketful of cash.

"Hey, sorry I'm so late. I had some business that needed my immediate attention," he stated as he sat down directly across from her. "How about we skip next period and work on my math?"

Tamara didn't want to cut her next class, but there was something about this guy that made it hard for her to say no. She didn't know whether it was his good looks, his bad-boy demeanor, how he always walked around like he ruled the world, or the way he smelled that made her feel all gushy inside. She was getting that wet feeling in her panties again as she watched him counting the money in his hand.

"Okay, but if you expect me to help you, you have to be here on time," Tamara demanded.

The whole time they sat there studying, Tamara kept thinking about how it would feel to kiss his nice lips. Between questions she would fade in and out, causing Ed to have to repeat his answer.

"Are you straight? You seem like you're not really here."

"Yeah! So if x equals 85, then what is the missing number in the equation?" Tamara asked, trying to change the subject.

He thought about the answer for a moment, wanting to make sure he answered correctly. Just as he was about to

answer, he received a text message. He pulled his cell phone out and read it.

"I have to go," he declared, jumping up and running out of the library, leaving his books on the table.

Tamara could sense something was wrong, but didn't know what. She gathered both of their books and headed out of the library. Since school was almost over, she headed outside to wait for her ride.

SEVEN

As soon as Akira walked through her door, she headed straight for the shower. She towel-dried her hair, threw on a pair of tights and a T-shirt, and then headed into her room to count the money she made last night. While sitting on her bed, it hit her that she hadn't heard from Jeff, and wondered if she was supposed to pick up Tamara and DJ today. She looked around for her purse so she could get her phone and call Tamara. When she didn't see it, she walked into the living room to see if she may have left it there.

"Fuck!" she cursed out loud.

She remembered that she left it back at the hotel. Her wallet, cell, and everything else was in there. As much as she didn't want to, she had to go back. She slipped on a pair of Reeboks, ready to head out the door. She flung the door open in a rush, and her entire body froze.

"You got a nigga driving all the way out here with all these white folks," Gene complained as he handed Akira her purse. "Better be glad I still love your ass."

He pushed his way past her and began looking around her junky but lavish crib. Akira clenched her jaws and gritted her teeth. She didn't need him knowing where she lived.

"Thanks for bringing it," she replied, looking through it to make sure everything was there. Jeff made himself

comfortable on the couch. "What are you doing?"

Jeff stretched his size thirteen shoes on her coffee table. "I'm making myself comfortable, baby." He leaned back and folded his hands behind his head. "I can get used to this, feel me?"

"Get your dirty shoes off my good shit!" She walked over to the table and pushed his feet off of the table.

"What's your problem, ma? A few hours ago we were all over each other, and now you trying to flip the script like you don't know me or something."

"My problem is, you think that I'm just supposed to drop everything I've built here and run back to you."

"Did I say that?"

"That's how you're making it seem," Akira told him.

"So all of a sudden, you think you're too good for me? Is that what it is?" Gene stared at Akira wide-eyed. "Is that what you're saying?"

He got up and slowly walked closer to where she was standing. He lifted her chin and turned her attention back to him.

"I want you back, and I will do everything in my power to make it happen."

"You keep on talking about us, but not once did you mention anything about your daughter. Why is that?" she asked, frustrated.

"I do want to see my daughter too. Maybe I can come

spend some time with her one day," he said, trying to throw her off his true intentions.

"You're such a liar," she said, twisting her lips and cutting her eyes at him.

"Look. I'ma keep it one hundred with you. I can't just stop being the person I am overnight. But, I will try to take it one step at a time."

Akira looked him in the eyes, and she knew he was at least telling the truth about that. She could feel it in her soul, but his charming manipulation wasn't going to work this time. Her cell phone started ringing. It was Jeff's ringtone.

"I have to get this," Akira said, about to walk away.

"Uh-uh. Whoever that is can wait," Gene said, trying to grip her ass.

"It's Jeff!"

He let her go, and before she could get her phone out of her purse, it stopped ringing. Seconds later, a text came through. It was Jeff again letting her know that he had picked the kids up and was on his way home. She needed to get rid of Gene before they arrived.

"He's on his way home, and I have to get ready for work. Where are you going to be later?" she asked.

"You mean you're going back to that fucking strip club?" he snapped.

"Akira drew her neck back and put one hand on her hip. "Damn right, because that fucking strip club," she shot with

an attitude, "is what pays my bills and feeds my kids."

"Take this," Gene said, pulling out money.

He peeled off a few hundred dollars and passed it to her. At first she wouldn't take it, but he wouldn't take no for an answer. She just needed him to leave before Jeff got home.

"What am I supposed to do with this?"

"It should hold you down for a couple of days."

Akira looked at the money and then back at Jeff. She burst out laughing hysterically, thinking he must be joking.

"Did you just say a couple of days? Please, I make this in an hour," she quipped, still laughing.

"I'm not fucking playing with you. If I catch you in that club, I will make your life as miserable as hell."

"Can you please leave, Gene?"

"I'm telling you, Akira, don't get fucked up; and tell my daughter that I will be back to see her," he whispered in her ear, then left out, leaving the door ajar.

Akira ran over and shut the door, locking it behind her. She took a deep breath to calm her nerves, then sat on the couch. She didn't know what to do and was scared as hell of Gene. If he said he would do something, he always did exactly what he said. She needed to work, but couldn't risk going back to Onyx because she was sure he would stop by. She had a couple of clients she could see, but that was just at the club. She decided she would just have to make some exceptions. Akira made a few calls to set up some things,

then hung up. Jeff and the kids walked in just as she finished.

"Mommy, Mommy, I had so much fun at school today," DJ said, running to his mother and hugging her leg.

"Did you now?" she replied. "Tell me what you did."

Tamara headed up to her room while they stayed in the living room bonding. She wanted to get out of her clothes and take a shower. After she undressed, she wrapped a towel around her, then headed into the bathroom. She turned on the water, checked the temperature, dropped her towel, and stepped inside. As she washed between her legs, the friction from her wash rag had her feeling good.

She imagined that it was Ed once again, touching her in her secret place. Her eyes were closed and the washcloth was putting in work. Just as her body was beginning to tense up, the bathroom door opened.

"Tamara, I have something to tell you," her mom said, ruining her fun. "Your father is here in Philly and would like to see you."

"Why? I don't want to see him, so please don't make me, Mom," she responded.

"I can't make you see him if you don't want to. I was just hoping you would give him a chance though, but like I said, it's up to you."

"Nope, he's dead to me. Now can I please finish taking my shower in peace?" she asked impatiently.

"Okay then! I have to work tonight, but if I'm not back

in time to take y'all to school and Jeff acts funny, call an Uber to take you. Is there anything special you want for dinner?"

"Maybe pizza. I don't know, Mom, ask DJ what he wants and we'll share. Now please leave so I can finish," Tamara said, trying to rush her mother out of the bathroom. Akira left and went back in the living room with her son and Jeff.

No longer feeling frisky, Tamara washed up again, then exited the shower. She went into her room, mad that her mom interfered with her daydream.

EIGHT

"Are you okay?"

"Yeah! I thought that was you," Kayla said, hugging her lil cousin. "Why did you send someone else to make the sale? This probably wouldn't have happened if you would have gone like you were supposed to."

"Then that would have been me being carried out in a body bag. That nigga will get his, don't worry about it."

"We just took a big losd, and I'm not really feeling that right now. Rico is going to still want his money in two days."

"I told you not to take shit on consignment, K. We was doing alright without all that extra shit. We are in a fucked-up situation," he said, sitting next to her on the couch. "What are we gonna do?"

"I'm going to call and go see him today. That way I won't be waiting tilll the last minute to tell him. I think he needs to know the truth. If that don't work, I'll give him the money I have put away and let him know that I'm working on the rest," she said.

"I will give you what I have also."

"No you won't," she protested. "That money is for college, and I wouldn't dare take that from you, so don't even think about it. I promised your mom that I would look out for you while she was in prison, and that's what I intend

on doing."

"I was only trying to help, Cuz."

"I will take care of it. I'm just hoping he understands and gives me a few more days," Kayla stated, getting up to grab some water. "So when will you be visiting that college?"

"Next month. They want me to come to one of their frat parties next weekend, but I don't know about that."

"I think you should go," she said, chopping ice up then putting it in a glass.

"Let's talk about this money right now because that's a big problem. Is there any way we can get at some of those niggas' bankrolls at your job?"

"Fuck no! Are you crazy? They will kill you and won't lose a wink of sleep. I told you to let me handle it, okay?"

"Alright, but I'm going to see if anybody saw that nigga Rajon. You sure he's the one that killed my homie?"

"Positive! He came over starting some shit, but a friend of mine was here and stopped him," she said, walking her cousin to the door. Her phone rang. It was Rico. "Hold on for a second. Hello?"

After talking for a couple of minutes, Kayla ended the call. She told her cousin that Rico wanted to meet with both of them now. She didn't know what to expect, so she ran up to her room and grabbed half of the money she had and threw it in a duffle bag. When she came back outside, her cousin was stuffing his gun in his waist.

"I'm ready!" he said.

"No, leave that in the car when we get there. They don't let no weapons inside."

Even though he didn't like it, he nodded his head in agreement as Kayla walked around and hopped in the passenger seat.

~ ~ ~

A tall man in his late forties leaned against the wall on the half-dark secluded block. His demeanor was calm, but his eyes were filled with rage. His partner, Herb, from the Richard Allen projects, leaned against the Mercedes. Herb was watching his partner closely because he knew how much of a time bomb he was. He was the only person that knew how to turn off Merv's kill switch, and was hoping that he wasn't about to do something crazy right now.

To the average person, they were just two executive businessmen, but those that knew them knew they were a force to be reckoned with. They were the heads of the most powerful drug organization in the city. Merv played the enforcer as well as the lieutenant position, while Herb was the boss. He wasn't your typical call-the-shots, point-the-finger kind of boss. He was more hands on because he liked drama. No one ever gave them any problems because they were very well connected, in high places. They even had

some law enforcement in their pockets.

Kayla stood there patiently waiting to see what was about to take place. When she arrived, they were already there. Standing next to her was her cousin, who stood there quietly, just allowing his cousin to plead her case. A group of men were also standing around with other intentions on their minds. They paced back and forth, waiting for the signal. Kayla started getting nervous after peeking over her shoulder and seeing them.

Herb became agitated. He raised up from the truck and finally spoke. "Your cousin is a grown-ass man. He's been in this game for a while now. Let him speak for himself," he said, before looking over into the young man's eyes. "The bottom line is this, you trusted one of your friends with my shit. Now he's dead and my shit is missing. Kayla, me and you have a rapport. I've been dealing with you ever since you first started stripping at my club, and that's the only reason we are standing here right now. When the word came back to us, our first thoughts were to slaughter your cousin, but because of you, we chilled."

"He's fucking lucky," Merv added, looking at Kayla's cousin, who stood there, eyes full of fear. "I think he should be the one who repays us, not her."

"I swear to God, the person that did this will pay with his life," Kayla's cousin said, speaking for the first time.

"Well, my next question is, who is this person? Give me

a name," Herb said, ice-grilling them.

They both stood there momentarily, waiting for Kayla to tell them the name of the person who robbed them.

"His name is Rajon," she blurted out.

Herb looked at them with menacing eyes. The only thing on his mind was murder, and that's exactly what was going to take place very soon. Even though they weren't familiar with the name, they knew people that would have the threat eliminated before he had a chance to spend a dime.

"Yo," Merv said to one of his men. He walked over to his boss, who whispered something to him, and then he left.

"I brought you something to show that we will get your stuff back," Kayla said, opening up the duffle bag and showing them the money.

"We don't want your money that came from popping your pussy," Merv said.

"What he means by that is, we don't want what you worked so hard to get," Herb cut in, trying to calm his partner down. "You're just gonna work extra hard to pay us back. Rico will still be overseeing all of the business, so contact him, because we hate coming here for nothing. Once your debt is paid in full, then and only then will we do business again. Are we clear?"

"Crystal," Kayla replied.

"Oh yeah, don't worry about this Rajon character. He'll be dead by tomorrow morning, and if my shit comes back

unhitched, then we may consider the debt paid," Merv stated, walking toward the opened car door.

"Just check the local news for updates," Herb said, backpedaling toward the car. He got into the backseat and closed the door. All their men stood there, staring coldly at Kayla and her cousin until their bosses' car pulled off down the street. Seconds later, they all jumped into the van they came in, and followed behind their bosses. The van cruised passed Kayla slowly, with the passenger sticking the assault rifle out the window, intensifying the fear in them, then sped off.

Later that night, sure enough, there was breaking news. Two bodies were found with multiple shots to the torso, and their hands were cut off. Police said the mutilated bodies were that of Rajon Reynolds and his cousin Raymond Turner. At that moment Kayla wished she'd have stuck to stripping. Now she was in way over her head and was just happy to still be breathing.

NINE

Akira was invited to a gathering with one of her clients. She had no choice since Gene had threatened to keep showing up at her job. This was the way she was going to keep getting money until she figured out a different plan. When she arrived, the place was lit. Everyone was dancing and having a good time. Akira spotted who she had been looking for and made her way over to greet him. When she got close, he looked up and smiled, glad to see her.

"Nice of you to come," he said, giving her a kiss on the cheek. "Please, have a seat."

"Thank you!" she said.

As they enjoyed each other's company, Akira noticed that one of the guests couldn't take his eyes off her. She had to admit that he looked very sexy to her. Every time she turned her head to say something to her friend, then looked over where the stranger was, he was still staring. To anyone else, that would be uncomfortable, but not to Akira. In fact, she was intrigued to know who he was.

When he started walking toward their table, Akira felt butterflies in her stomach. She knew her friend might get jealous. But instead of stopping, the guy walked right past as if he didn't see her, and headed over to the bar area.

"I have to do a little meet and greet. I'll be back in a few

minutes. Since you like dancing, why don't you hit the dance floor, and I'll join you when I'm done."

Akira nodded her head as her friend made his way over to some of his associates. She sat there sipping on her drink until she heard someone behind her speak.

"Would you like to dance?"

"Sure," Akira said, as he led her out to the crowded dance floor.

As they danced to the slow song, he rubbed his dick up against her pelvis. It seemed like the more they danced, the harder he became. Akira was even becoming aroused from his touch. By time the song was over, her panties were soaked. He walked her back over to the table.

"Your lady friend is very beautiful, and can really dance," he said to Akira's date.

"I hope you weren't trying to steal my date," he said to the man.

"No, he was the perfect gentleman," Akira chimed in, interrupting them.

"Why don't you have a seat and join us for a drink? My name is Rico," he said, extending his hand out to shake the man's hand.

"I'm Eric, but my friends call me E," he said, accepting his invitation.

They were sitting in a U-shaped booth, and Eric brazenly sat down next to Akira and started up a conversation with

Rico. Every chance he got, he tried to flirt with her. He even went so far as placing his hand on her leg and rubbing it. Akira could feel the electricity shooting through her body. Another song came on that she liked, so she asked Rico to dance with her. She wanted to get away from this tempting man.

"I have to go talk to some more business associates. Why don't you dance with her for me again. This meeting can't wait." Rico got up and excused himself from the table, leaving the two of them there.

"Well, shall we?" E said, standing up, holding his hand out to her.

Reluctantly, she took it and followed him back onto the dance floor. He once again got her so horny that she purposely rubbed the tip of his dick with the back of her hand.

"Why don't we walk outside and get some air?" he suggested.

Akira didn't even hesitate this time, wanting to go and be alone with him. She hoped Rico wasn't watching them. He took her by the hand and led her out to the parking lot. Eric led her over to where he parked his car, which was in a secluded area of the lot. He pulled her to him, and they kissed, leaning on the front of the car. His hands explored her whole body, caressing her breasts, pinching her nipples, causing her entire body to shudder with pleasure. At this

point, she didn't care who was watching them. Akira reached between Eric's legs and rubbed his dick. She was unprepared for the size of it.

Eric lifted up her dress, then caressed her ass. Then he pulled off her panties at the same time she was unbuckling his pants. She removed his erection and held it in her hand. Even though it was dark, there was no mistaking that he was well endowed down there. He sat her on the edge of the car and guided his erection between her legs.

She held her dress out of the way and watched in the dim lighting as it rubbed her clit. Akira rocked her hips back and forth, in an effort to have him penetrate her swollen cunt, but he had other ideas. He continued to move his dick across her soaked pussy, teasing her into her first orgasm.

"Oh shit, yeeesss," she moaned as she coated the frame of his car with her juices.

Eric smiled and began pushing his dick inside her, filling her up. Lifting her off the car, he started moving in rhythmic strokes. Their skin slapped together each time they moved. Suddenly, he tensed up and pulled out, as his dick erupted, leaving his semen all over the ground.

"Damn, ma, we definitely have to do that again," Eric said, kissing her gently on the lips.

They walked back into the club like nothing happened. Akira's legs were shaky and she felt her cum still leaking into her panties. She needed to use the bathroom to clean up.

"Excuse me while I use the ladies' room."

"Here, take my number, just in case you want to maybe have a nightcap," he replied, storing his number in her phone. "If you're not going to use it, delete it."

"Don't worry about that," she stated, making her way through the crowd, knowing she wasn't.

She eased past all the females waiting outside of the ladies' room and slid inside. After removing her panties, she cleaned up and headed out to find Rico. He was talking to a couple of women by the bar. Akira felt a bit of jealousy as she approached the group.

"You ready to go?" he asked, giving her a peck on the lips.

"Yes," she said, happy that he showed them he was taken.

On the ride home, Akira's pussy was still on fire. That quickie she had with Eric was nothing more than a tease. She needed the fire between her legs put out. Rico never asked her where she dipped off to or anything. He was too busy talking on the phone to someone. If he was angry, she couldn't tell. He was quiet all the way back to the hotel.

Once they were in the room, Akira wanted to take a shower to freshen up for the long night ahead of them.

"Where did you go?" he asked, sitting his phone on the table.

"What do you want to know?" she asked. She moved

close to him on the bed, putting her hand on his penis and massaging it. "Do you want to know where I was, or do you want to know where I'm about to go? Maybe you want to know how wet my pussy is right now for you."

Rico had a shocked look on his face, but his dick sprang to life. Akira took his hand and placed it between her legs. He began rubbing her clit slowly. She pushed him back onto the bed, climbed on top of him, and unbuttoned his pants. Usually he was the one who initiated sex, but now she was the aggressor. She pulled her dress over her head and inched up till her pussy was inches from his face.

"I want you to eat me, Rico. I want you to see how wet you made me."

Akira covered his mouth with her body. His tongue darted between her pussy lips, in search of her G-spot.

"Mmmmmmm," he moaned.

"Can you taste how wet I am?" She asked.

Rico could only groan as Akira grinded her pussy on his face. Feeling her muscles tightening up, he moved his tongue harder and faster around her box. She wondered if he could taste Eric's pre cum, even though she tried to wash it away. He felt her about to bust, so he slowed up his pace.

"Don't stop," she said, and Rico continued eating her pussy until he was drinking her milk.

She rolled off his face and lay on her back, sticking two fingers inside her twat, waiting for him to fuck her brains

out.

"Come on!"

Still wet with anticipation, Akira opened her legs as wide as they could go as he explored her body with his hands and eyes. He started kissing her neck and chest. His penis grew incredibly hard as it entered her. He started off slow, then sped up the pace.

"Yessss, fuck me, baby," she screamed out in pleasure.

Akira pushed him off of her, then got down between his legs. She swirled her tongue around the head of his dick. She could only get half of him in her mouth. She became so excited that he had to tell her to slow down. Her head game was better than Superhead's.

"Slow down, baby, or I'm gonna explode in your mouth," he yelled.

When she didn't, he pulled her up and kissed her. She felt his dick pressing up against her wetness, and moved into a squatting position, and then with her right hand guided it into position. Akira was so wet with her own juices that his dick easily entered her hole. Slowly she impaled herself on his shaft. With both hands on his chest for balance, she began pumping up and down on his anaconda. Seeing it disappear inside her was electrifying. Rico was cupping and squeezing her titties.

"God, you have beautiful titties, and you make me feel so good," he said, getting emotional. "I just might be falling

for you."

She suddenly became alarmed. She knew her pussy was addictive, but, "Damn, now he's falling in love," she thought. He placed his thumb on her swollen clit and massaged it vigorously. Her body rocked in an explosive orgasm.

"I'mmmm cuuummmmin," she moaned, trembling uncontrollably.

A couple of minutes later, Rico shot his load also. Akira collapsed on his chest and squeezed her legs together in order to milk the last drops of cum out of him.

"Finish me off, baby. Suck this dick until I'm hard again."

Slipping down his sweaty body, Akira pulled back the foreskin of his semi-erect dick and licked his head around the tip. Gazing up, she could see that he was enjoying her performance.

She licked the cum from his dick and then sucked him until he was fully erect again. She stood up and placed her breast in his mouth.

"Shhhh, suck it, baby," she said softly.

Rico uttered a low moan. She eased him onto his back again, then positioned herself so that her pussy was directly over his face. If there was anything she loved more than dick, it was getting her pussy eaten.

"You know what to do."

Rico's tongue darted between the lips of her pussy, tentatively at first, then he started going hard to bring her to yet another monstrous orgasm. She didn't waste any time taking him in her mouth either. They stayed in the sixty-nine position until they both released into each other's mouths. By the time they fell asleep, they were both exhausted. A bomb could have exploded right next to them and they wouldn't have heard it.

The next day Akira rushed home knowing that she had been fucking up by staying out with her customers. She had broken her own rule and was starting to feel guilty about it. That was until she counted the three grand she made from Rico. Jeff wasn't even home when she got there. She took a shower, then lay across her bed naked and fell asleep.

TEN

Tamara had been seeing a lot of Ed lately. They met every afternoon to study, and he even suggested that she should dress like a female. He told her how beautiful she was if she just showed it off to everybody. Of course, she brushed it off as she always did. They made a bet that if he passed his test on Friday, she would go to the frat party with him and she would wear something girly. She agreed to it, but the catch was, he had to get nothing less than an A.

They arrived at class on Monday, and Ed sat at his desk anxiously waiting his test paper. It wasn't because of the bet, but because it would get his average up to go to the college of his choice. Tamara wasn't a slouch when it came to school, so she did not hold back tutoring Ed. She thought he was just a class clown that didn't pay attention. He just wanted to impress the rest of the class with his practical jokes. When she first started tutoring him, it was just a schoolgirl crush, but now after getting to know the real Edward, she was really starting to like him.

"Okay, class, these test results were very impressive for some, and for others, you need to pay more attention in class instead of playing on your phones," the teacher said, passing out their graded test. The whole time he was talking, his eyes were on Ed.

Tamara assumed that he had failed, which meant he was

wasting her time. When their teacher gave him his test, the look on his face confirmed her suspicions.

"If you concentrate on your assignment, you will pass next week," Tamara whispered, trying not to disrupt the class.

"I can't believe this," Ed said, continuing to stare at his test paper. He looked up at Tamara and smiled. "I got an A+."

Tamara was taken back by the sudden chain of events. She knew what that meant, and inside she was excited to be going with him, but also nervous because she didn't know what to wear.

"I'll see you Friday," Ed said as they walked out of class.

Tamara just smiled because she had made a deal with the devil, and now she was going to a party she knew her mother wouldn't let her go to. When she saw her friend Tiffany at lunch, an idea popped into her head, and she suddenly decided to use her best friend as a cover.

"Hey, Tamara," Tiffany said, sitting across from her at the table.

"Hey, Tiff! I have a problem."

"What happened now?" Tiffany questioned, knowing more gossip was on its way.

"I told Ed I would go with him to a party, but I don't have anything to wear."

"All those clothes you have in your closet, girl, what are you talking about? Let's go to your house after school so we

can pick out something."

"There's more. I need to use you as an alibi just in case my mom asks where I'm gonna be. Can I say that I'll be at your place?"

"Of course you can, girl. Stop playing," Tiff replied. "Shit, I wish I could go with you."

"Maybe you can. I don't want to be there alone with strangers. If you go, I'll have someone to talk to besides Ed."

"Isn't your birthday Saturday?" Tiffany smiled. Tamara nodded her head yeah. "We really have to celebrate."

"That's a bet! I'll see you after school," Tamara said as they headed back to class. Tamara was happy she would be going on a date finally. Now she couldn't wait till Friday.

~ ~ ~

After picking up her son, Akira came home to an empty home. Once again Jeff wasn't home. He had been gone ever since she told him he needed to start doing something while he was there. Their son didn't deserve to be placed in the middle of such a dysfunctional family, but he was. She never for one moment regretted her decision to keep any of her children, but she did question the people she had them by. However, she did love him, and he loved her. He was just mad right now.

"Mom, can I have some milk and cookies, please?" DJ asked.

"Sure!" Akira replied, heading into the kitchen.

After she set the snack on the table, she went into the living room and flopped on the couch. She glanced at the clock on the wall and wondered when Jeff was going to come home. She laid her head, which was covered in a scarf, back against the pillow. Thoughts of what Gene had told her flooded her brain. She didn't understand why he could be so selfish and inconsiderate. She'd be damned if she was going to sit at home depending on any man.

Then back to Jeff, who despite her sneaking around fucking different men at the club, loved her and let her do what she needed to. She sometimes, like at this moment, felt needy and desperate for his attention. She was stuck between two men, and it wasn't fair. She was so tired of trying to rationalize her misplaced feelings. She wanted to find out where Jeff was so they could talk about what camp they would be sending their son to this summer.

Reluctantly, Akira picked up her cell phone and called Jeff. She really didn't know what she would end up saying, but was hoping to be in one accord with him, especially when it came to DJ. His phone went straight to voicemail.

"Jeff, this is me, your baby momma. Me and your son haven't heard from you, and I wanted to make sure you're okay." She rested her head on one arm and continued her message. "I wasn't going to work tonight so that we could spend time together. Let me know if you're coming home."

She ended the call and set the phone next to her. As if on

cue, Jeff's ringtone sounded off. She answered on the second ring.

"I was hoping that we could talk—" Akira couldn't finish what she was saying because of the angelic moaning of a woman's voice, soaring through the earpiece. "Hello," she uttered, sitting up.

Akira took a deep breath, pressed her lips together, and tried to stomach that perturbed feeling resting in the pit of her stomach.

"That's right, daddy. Fuck me harder!" the woman screamed.

The loud grunts were all too familiar to Akira. She called out Jeff's name. Her breathing was jagged and shallow. The words that came to mind were unexpectedly clogged in her throat.

"Whose pussy is this?" Akira heard Jeff ask the woman.

"It's yours, daddy!"

Akira ended the call, then leaned back on the couch, trying to catch her breath. It felt as though the air had been knocked out of her lungs. She couldn't believe what she had just heard. It felt like her heart had been ripped from her chest. Her body stiffened, and her fists were balled tightly at her sides. All the shit she was doing behind his back had done a 180. Karma was a bitch! She realized at that moment that as long as she was in this life, she would never have a true relationship.

ELEVEN

Friday had come so fast, and Tamara was nervous about going to the party. At least she had her best friend with her.

"Tamara, come on so I can see how you look," Tiffany said.

They were at Tiffany's house getting ready, since she told her mom she would be staying over her friend's house for the night. Akira wanted her to watch her brother, but after a little whining and a lot of persuasion, she was able to get out of it. She walked out of the bathroom, and Tiffany couldn't believe her eyes.

"How do I look?" Tamara asked.

"I'd fuck you," Tiffany joked. "Matter fact, I would eat the shit out of your pussy, girl. You are so fucking hot."

"Stop playing, Tiff," Tamara replied, acting shy.

"Who said I was playing? Seriously, he is going to be drooling all over when he sees you," Tiff told her as they headed downstairs.

Tamara had finally come out of her shell. She was rocking an all-black strapless Christian Dior pencil dress, with three-inch stilettos. The dress fitted so tight that it looked like it was painted on her Beyoncé figure. If you thought Akira was bad, she didn't have anything on her

daughter. Tiffany had flat-ironed her hair, and it came down just above her ass.

"So you think he will like it?"

"Hell yeah!" Tiff responded, licking her lips. Tamara didn't know it, but Tiffany was bisexual. So when she was trying to flirt with her, she meant it. "Let me hurry up before your friend gets here to pick us up."

Tiffany started putting on her makeup and fixing her hair. She also looked sexy in her Versace dress. Her hair was cut short and came to her shoulders. The two women were definitely dressed to impress thanks to Tiffany. Tamara was hoping Ed liked the new her. It was actually the first time since she was five years old that she had worn a dress.

"Beep, Beep!"

"Come on, Tiff, Ed is here," Tamara yelled from the door.

When Ed saw Tamara and Tiffany walk out the door, his dick instantly got hard. He had never seen anyone look as beautiful as Tamara was right now. He could see why she always wore baggy clothes to school. Tamara had an hourglass figure, and that tight dress she had on only proved what he was thinking: that she was unbelievable.

After telling them how beautiful they both were, they all hopped in his car and headed to the party at Lincoln University. Every chance he got, he would look over at Tamara. She looked nothing like the girl that sat in front of

him in class. When he checked his rearview mirror, Tiffany would sneakily lick her lips in a seductive manner at him. They listened to a variety of music on the way to the college trying to get hyped up for the party.

"We're not overdressed, are we?" Tiffany asked, making conversation.

"Hell no. There might be people there with nothing on." He smiled. "But seriously, did y'all bring bathing suits for the pool party?"

"No! We didn't know anything about that," Tamara replied.

"That's cool. We'll see what we can find for y'all when we get there." Ed was just hoping for a chance to get Tamara out of her dress so he could see her body up close and personal.

By the time they arrived, the party was lit. Everyone was enjoying themselves, dancing and getting drunk. Tamara felt like she was at her mother's club the way people were dressed. She realized that maybe they were a bit overdressed.

"Wow! We're at a college party, Tamara," Tiffany said with excitement.

"What would you ladies like to drink?" Ed asked.

"Anything!" they both said simultaneously, unsure of what they wanted.

Ed walked off, and they stood there watching people damn near fucking on the dance floor. This was truly a

different scene for Tamara, and she didn't know how to adjust to it. A few guys came up to her, asking to dance, but she politely declined. Tiffany, on the other hand, was quick to accept the offer.

"I'll be back, okay?" Tiff told her, walking off with some college dude.

Tamara watched her friend and the stranger tearing the floor down. Ed returned with their drinks and passed one to her.

"This should loosen you up a bit," he said.

Unbeknownst to either of the women, Ed had slid a couple of mollies in both of their drinks. She started sipping on the fruity-tasting drink. Ed smiled when she drank it like it was juice. Tiffany came back after a couple of songs and tasted her drink also.

"Damn, this tastes like fruit punch."

"Ed said it's called a 'Jamaican Me Happy,'" Tamara replied.

"Well I need another one."

"Me too!"

"I'll be right back," Ed said, heading over to the table where the drinks were. He wasn't trying to leave Tamara alone too long with all those thirsty, horny college guys. She was his for the night, hopefully. He just had to play his part for the night and hope things went his way.

~ ~ ~

Later that night everyone was enjoying themselves drinking and having fun. The party had already moved into the pool. Tamara had three drinks, and the molly had her and Tiffany feeling bold as ever. They had shed their clothing and jumped into the pool with just their panties and bras on. Ed was in awe at how good Tamara looked with no clothes on.

"Can you get me another drink?" Tamara asked.

"You sure? I don't think you need another one," Tiffany said, looking around for Ed to let him know they were ready to go.

Tamara was so fucked up that she passed out by the pool. Tiffany helped her over to a chair to rest. She saw Ed and signaled for him to come over. Tamara was passed out. There was no way he would be getting at her tonight, because she was tore up. He definitely wasn't going to try and take advantage of a helpless woman.

"I'm not ready to leave yet. She can lay in my cousin's room and sleep it off until we're ready."

Tiffany wasn't trying to leave either, so she agreed with Ed. They helped Tamara up to his cousin's dorm room and onto the bed. Ed couldn't keep his eyes off her camel toe poking through her panties. His erection was on full display.

"Let's go back to the party and finish having some fun," Tiffany said, walking toward the door.

She kept making her ass bounce to get Ed's attention. He

noticed and couldn't take his eyes off the way it swallowed up the french-cut panties she had on. He glanced at Tamara, then back at Tiffany. Most of the girls there only wore panties and bras, but Tiffany was the one he wanted now, since Tamara was sleep.

She was feeling frisky from the molly Ed had put in her drink. She didn't even know that it wasn't the liquor she was drinking that made her feel this way. Once they were back at the party, Ed sat on the couch to roll a Dutch.

"Let me get some of that," Tiffany said, sitting next to him. She smoked some of the Dutch, and it intensified the molly, making her feel even better. "This shit has me horny, how about you?"

"Watching you and Tamara walking around like that made me horny."

"Well are you planning to do anything about it?" She giggled.

"Maybe," he said laughing. He wasn't sure if she was just fucking with him, or if she really wanted to fuck him. "What about your friend?"

"If you don't tell, I won't tell," she whispered over the loud music.

"Let's go somewhere private," he said, pulling her up and leading her into another dorm where no one was. They sat on the bed, with Tiffany sitting really close to him.

"Why don't you tell me exactly what you want.," she

said. "Then we can take it from there."

"What I want? What I want is to eat that ass and sample that pussy," he replied, letting her know he was a freak.

"Let me see you go for it then," she said. "I'd like to see how good you really are."

"Whatever you want, baby," Ed said, getting excited.

She didn't look surprised at all that he would jump at the chance for some pussy. She had heard plenty of stories around school about him. She took a long drag off the Dutch, held it in, and slowly exhaled. Then she stood up, bent at the waist, and backed her ass up against his face, rubbing the bottom of her soaked panties against his mouth.

He wasn't about to waste any time letting her change her mind. He whipped her panties down to her thighs, and she was standing there naked from the waist down. Ed put his hands on her cheeks to spread them wide. He ran his tongue around the rim of her ass, then pushed it deep inside her hole.

"Ugh, yessss! What the fuck are you doing to me?" she moaned.

Ed just kept licking while she made little sighing sounds, letting him know she was enjoying what he was doing. He was so turned on by the taste and smell of her ass that it felt like his head was about to explode.

"I need to get up in there," he said, moving back momentarily.

She stepped out of her panties, then removed her bra. Ed

quickly removed his shorts and boxers. Tiffany knelt on the mattress on all fours, waiting for him to enter. He grabbed the condom out of his pocket and slid it on. Her ass was stuck in the air, inviting him to do as he pleased.

"Come on," she begged impatiently.

He got behind her, leveling the tip of his dick to her opening, pushing into her tight, wet pussy slowly, amazed by the warmth and feeling.

"Damn, you're so tight."

"Oh yeah," she groaned as he started moving in and out of her. "That feels so damn good! Now beat this pussy up before I get mad."

That's exactly what he did, too. He gripped her waist and went to work, trying to knock her walls out. She screamed out in pleasure and pain, clawing at the sheets and grunting in satisfaction until she felt him tensing up. She quickly turned around and pulled off his condom, then placed his dick into her mouth. She sucked until he exploded.

"Shit, yes!" Ed said as she swallowed his semen with no problem.

She stroked him until he had nothing left. They lay there until Ed was hard again. Then Tiffany got on top of him and started riding him. Instead of her getting dressed and checking on her friend, she wanted another round.

~ ~ ~

Tamara was still out of it as three dudes snuck into the room she was in. They stood over her, staring at her half-naked body. Ed's cousin thought someone had left him a gift when he walked into his room. He called his two friends to join in on the party. One of them removed the panties she was wearing, exposing her pretty pussy lips. The second dude spread her legs wide, while the third one stuck his face in between and started licking her sweet spot.

She began to moan, feeling a sensation coming over her. Expecting it to be Ed, Tamara opened her eyes. Horror suddenly hit her when she saw one dude between her legs and two more standing over her with their dicks out. Soon as she tried to scream, one of the dudes covered her mouth.

"Shhhhhh! I thought you wouldn't mind doing all of us," he whispered with a sinister smirk.

Tamara didn't know what to do as the men took turns having their way with her. She tried to call out to Tiffany, but no one could hear her muffled cries because her mouth was covered. The football jocks were so drunk they didn't care that they were sexually assaulting an underage girl.

The more they raped her, the wetter she got, and the more numb she became. Her body kept jerking uncontrollably, which made them think she liked it. In all reality, she was having orgasms she couldn't control. Tears came down her face as she lay there wishing it would all be over.

"Hurry up so I can get another turn," one of the dudes

that was holding her arms said. They switched after the other one nutted all over her stomach.

The mollies that Ed had slipped her earlier were what had her body responding like that, but she didn't know it. The blood on the bed from them popping her cherry only egged them on. Tamara closed her eyes and dreamed she was in a far-off place, at the same time praying Tiffany and Ed would come save her.

~ ~ ~

Ed and Tiffany had just finished another round of steamy hot sex and were getting dressed before whoever's room they were in came back.

"Let's go get Tamara and get her home. I have to get our clothes first," Tiffany said as they headed toward the pool. "Tamara can never find out about this okay?"

"I was going to say the same thing. My keys are in her purse, right?"

"Yeah! Here," she said, passing him his keys.

They headed to his cousin's room to get Tamara. When Tiffany opened the door, her friend was lying in the fetal position crying. Her underclothes were balled up in her hand, and blood was all over the bed. She jumped, thinking the boys were coming back for more.

"Leave me alone," she yelled.

"Oh my God, Tamara, what happened to you?" Tiffany said, rushing to her friend.

"I tried to call you, but they covered my mouth. I didn't know what to do."

Ed quickly looked in the closet and grabbed a shirt and some sweatpants for Tamara to put on. He was pissed that he had left her alone like that for a quickie. He looked at Tiffany, who also had guilt all over her face.

"Who did this to you, Tamara?" Ed asked. "Somebody is going to fucking pay for this." Tamara pointed to the picture on the wall. It was a picture of his cousin. Ed's eyes turned black as anger overclouded his better judgment. "Get her the fuck out of here now and take her to the car. Turn it on, and wait for me." He passed Tiffany the keys to his car then left the room.

"Come on, baby, we have to go now," Tiffany said, knowing something bad was about to happen.

Ed was furious as he walked through the house looking for his cousin. He saw him with two of his buddies, standing outside, talking to some chicks. He walked out of the house and approached the group of boys. Without saying a word, he punched his cousin dead in the nose. His cousin fell backward, hitting his head on the wall.

"What the f—" one of his friends was about to say, but was met with a .40 cal aimed at his face.

"Give me a reason, you bitch-ass nigga." He turned and

looked at his cousin, who was still holding his nose. "Why the fuck did you rape my friend?"

"Cuz, I don't know what you're talking about. I didn't rape anybody." He was so scared that he pissed on himself. The other two guys didn't say a word.

"Don't fucking lie to me, nigga. She told me it was you."

"You can ask them. We were together all night," he replied, pointing to his friends.

Ed was about to say something, until he heard footsteps approaching from behind. When he turned to look, it was Tamara and Tiffany.

"I told y'all to wait for me in the car."

"They raped me," Tamara said, pointing to all three of the men.

"All three of them?" Ed asked. When Tamara nodded her head, Ed snapped, shooting all three men in the chest, not even caring who saw him.

People that were outside watching the confrontation started scattering and running for cover. In the background, you could hear the campus police cars zooming up the block. Ed had nowhere to run. Tamara quickly grabbed the gun from him and stuffed it in her sweatpants, between her legs.

"Put your hands up now!" the officers stated, jumping out of the car with their guns drawn.

Tamara and Tiffany watched as they locked Ed up and hauled him off to the police station to be booked and

processed. The three men were rushed to the hospital, where they would later be listed in critical but fair condition.

"Are you okay?" Tiffany asked, looking at her friend as she drove Ed's car back home.

"I just want to go home," she replied, looking out the window.

She was sore, scared, and worried about Ed. She couldn't believe he just shot three people and went to jail, trying to protect her. She was going to do whatever it took to help get him out of there.

"Tamara, I think you should stay at my house tonight. Your mom finds out what happened, and she will snap out." Tiffany stated. She felt like shit for leaving her friend in a vulnerable state while she went and fucked her man. That hurt her more than anything.

"We have to get rid of this gun," Tamara said. They pulled over near a lake, and she tossed it in there. Then they headed to Tiffany's without saying another word about it.

TWELVE

Eric walked out of his Karmen Suites apartment, heading for his car. The area was quiet, just a few stragglers moving along their way. As he hit the alarm button on his key ring, his attention was caught by the loud screeching of tires behind him. He turned around and was greeted by the barrel of a handgun hanging out the passenger's window of a black utility van. Before he could make a move to run or anything else, the side door burst opened, and a man with dreads hopped out, gun in hand.

"Get the fuck in the van," the man shouted.

Eric had his hands raised high in the air in submission, thinking it was a robbery. The man grabbed him by the collar and tossed him inside the van, slamming the door behind him. They sped off without anyone noticing what had happened.

"Where are you taking me?" Eric asked.

"Shut the fuck up," the dread-headed man said, smacking him across the head with the butt of the gun.

~ ~ ~

Eric lay in the corner of the dark abandoned apartment, curled up, as he was being stomped out abusively. Finally

Gene stepped up and commanded his men to stop the abuse. Eric peeked up through his arms that he used as a shield and stared into the barrel of a semiautomatic handgun.

"Please," he cried. "Please. I told y'all I had no idea she was married. She came to the club with one of my business partners. I thought she was just another chick that he brought along like he usually does. I didn't ask any questions about if she was taken or not. Come on, man, you gonna put my life on the line for a piece of pussy?"

"Your life isn't on the line," Gene said, as he cocked the chamber back. "Your life is over. That is unless you can give me the rundown of that club you work at." Gene chuckled because Eric thought this was over a bitch, but Gene actually wanted to rob the club.

"What about the club?" he asked, dumbfounded.

"I want you to tell me everything I need to know, like where the safe is and the best time to run up in there."

Eric knew it would be a suicide mission trying to rob Herb and Merv. He would rather die than have to deal with them for betraying their trust. A small group of people including Eric had a small share in Onyx, but Merv and Herb were the majority owners.

"I'm just in charge of hiring security," he lied. "I don't deal with the money at all. Rico is the one that handles that part. I swear, man, I'm not lying to you."

Gene stood there deep in thought. For some reason that

name kept coming up, but he couldn't figure out why.

"Rico, Rico," he said slowly. "Why does that name sound familiar to me?"

"If you ever copped any dope out here, you got it from him," Eric said. "Please, I'll do anything you want. Just don't kill me."

"Is that right?" Gene said, coming up with an idea. "I have a better plan, and you're gonna help me pull it off."

Gene looked over at his man Maurice who was standing shoulder to shoulder with him. Gene paused for a minute or so, and thought before speaking. When Gene whispered something to him, he nodded his head in agreement. He dug into his pocket, and retrieved Eric's cell phone. He handed it to Eric.

"Here, take it," Maurice said. Eric hesitantly reached for the phone, not trusting him.

"Call your man and tell him you need more of the dope," Gene commanded. "When he gets here, you're gonna knock his shit off in front of us. Now call him." Gene nudged Eric's head with his gun.

Eric knew this was his only chance to warn his peoples, and dialed the number with no hesitation. "Put him on speaker," Maurice whispered. Eric hit the speaker button after he pressed send.

Once he finished, they waited with anticipation filling their guts. A delayed ring sounded off before the operator

came on: "We're sorry, the number you have reached is no longer in service."

Eric looked at the phone with confusion before quickly dialing again. The automated service came on again. Eric looked up at Gene with a terrified look in his eyes.

Boom!

Eric's body fell backward. Before his back touched the ground, Gene fired three more shots.

Boom! Boom! Boom!

The four shots to the face left holes the size of lemons. Gene used his foot to sway Eric's head to the side. He stared into his eyes, and even though he was still breathing, Gene saw death in them. He squeezed one more time, aiming at the center of his forehead. He hadn't had to put in work in almost fifteen years and just wanted to test his aim to see if he still had it. He mashed the trigger one more time for good measure. The bullet spun out of the barrel and landed right between his eyebrows. Gene smiled with satisfaction knowing he still had it.

THIRTEEN

It had been a week since the incident with Tamara happened. She was still healing, and her best friend never left her side. Tamara made Tiffany promise she wouldn't say anything to anybody, not even her mom. If her mom found out what happened, Tamara would never be able to go out anywhere.

They had called around and found out Ed's bail was a hundred thousand dollars, and he needed 10 percent to get out. He was charged with three counts of attempted murder. Tamara was determined to help him, even if she had to do the unthinkable to get the money. He was in there for taking up for her, and she was thankful for it. She was even ready to rob somebody, when Kayla came up with an idea to help them out. They never told her the real reason he was there, just that he took up for them when some boys were messing with them.

"I have some checks I got from work. If y'all cash them for me, you can keep enough to get your friend out, and I'll take the rest. Tamara, under no circumstances can you tell your mother, got it?" Tamara nodded her head. "Okay, I'm going to take y'all to the bank, and all you have to do is give the check to the teller and wait for the money."

"Where you gonna be?" Tiffany asked her sister.

"I'll will be right there with you. This is the fastest money you can make right now to help out your friend."

Tiffany was really feeling guilty about what she had done. She didn't think her friend was really into Ed like that. But Tamara was willing to risk her freedom trying to save another. That was what influenced Tiffany to rock with Tamara no matter what. Besides that, the guilt trip was tearing her up inside.

"Can we do it now, so we can get Ed out?" Tamara asked. She was anxious to handle her business. "What if they're hurting him in there?" She didn't know how prison was, except for what her dad told her when he wrote her.

"I just have to write the amount on them, and then we can go," Kayla said, heading upstairs to retrieve the checks.

~ ~ ~

"Ewww-wee, girl, all these bourgeois bitches up in here," Tiffany said as they walked through the Bank of America lobby.

All eyes were on them because they were all looking fly as hell. Tamara was even starting to dress like a woman now. She was rocking a red and white tennis skirt with a matching shirt, and a pair of Jordans, courtesy of Tiffany and Kayla.

Tamara walked ahead feeling as if she was the bank's president. Both women and men stopped and stared at their asses as they walked by. They stood in line, and when the

two available tellers called them up, they each went to separate windows.

"How may I help you?" the cheerful young dark-skinned girl asked. She had some of the biggest cheeks Tamara had ever seen, but the most beautiful dimples.

"Hello, I came to cash my settlement check," Tamara said, remembering what Kayla told her to say. She handed the woman a personal check written in the amount of $15,000 dollars.

The teller looked over the check carefully then looked up at Tamara, maintaining her friendly customer service smile. "Ms. Moses, may I have your right thumb print here."

Tamara placed her thumb on the ink pad, then stuck her print on the check. She passed it back through the window.

"Do you have two forms of identification?"

"Yes, I do."

Tamara handed the teller her state ID and her school ID. She also pulled out her social security card and handed it to the teller just in case.

The teller studied them closely. "Thank you!" She began typing away on her computer, and as she did, Tamara looked over at Tiffany to see how things were going on her end. She could hear the teller asking her for the same kind of identification.

"Ms. Moses, how would you like your cash back?" the teller asked, smiling.

Tamara tried to hold back the excitement she was

feeling. All she could think about was getting her possible boyfriend out of prison.

"Whatever's easiest for you," she said politely.

"Okay, Ms. Moses. I'll have to step to the back to get your cash, but I will be right back."

"Okay, take your time," Tamara said. "I'll be right here."

"Please help yourself to some coffee and cookies while you're waiting. We're also running a great promotion. If you open up a checking account with us today, you'll get two months of free check writing."

"I'll think about it," she said as she made her way to the lobby. Shortly after, Tiffany followed.

"Bitch, we are about to get paid!" Tiffany said the second she sat down.

"Sshhh! They're gonna hear your loudmouth ass."

Tiffany quickly placed a hand over her mouth. She was just excited that they picked this easy way to get some money.

"My bad! I'll be back, I have to use the bathroom. It's that time of the month."

"Remember, we have to go get him out of there today," Tamara said, worried. "Hurry your ass up, girl. They should be coming back out with our money in a minute."

Tiffany picked up her purse and dashed off to change her tampon, while Tamara sat there patiently waiting for her money. She calculated how much would be left after they paid Ed's bail and Kayla took her cut. If everything went as

planned, she was going to turn this into her hustle.

When Tiffany returned, they waited for fifteen more minutes, before they realized it was taking too long.

"What the hell is taking them so long?" Tamara wondered.

"I don't know. Go see, Tamara."

Tamara tossed the napkin and coffee cup in the trashcan before walking over to the teller's window to ask what the holdup was. The teller was nowhere in sight, so Tamara asked the other teller what was taking so long.

"Let me check for you, ma'am."

"Thank you very much," Tamara said, disguising her frustration.

The teller returned rather quickly and informed her that they were still counting the money and would be out in a couple more minutes. Satisfied with the answer, Tamara nodded her head then walked back over to where Tiffany was.

"They're counting the money," she told her.

"Damn, it takes that long? Don't they have one of those machines that counts money for you? I wish they would come on, it feels like something ain't right."

Tamara looked at her as if she was crazy. She was acting as if the cops were about to come storming in at any second. Another ten minutes passed before the tellers came back out.

"Ms. Moses," Tamara's teller called out.

"Ms. Jenkins," the other teller who was helping Tiffany

said.

"About damn time," Tiffany huffed under her breath. They walked over to the windows, and there was no money in sight.

"Ms. Moses, I'm sorry to inform you that we are unable to cash your check today."

"What! Why is that?" Tamara asked disappointedly.

"Because those checks are stolen. So for that reason, we're going to have to retain them as evidence."

"I didn't steal any checks. There has to be some kind of mistake!" Tamara exclaimed.

"Evidence!" Tiffany said, getting nervous.

When they heard the lobby door chirp, they both turned around to find two Philadelphia police officers walking inside.

"Fuck," Tiffany hissed under her breath.

"Tiff, I can't go to jail. My mom will kill me," Tamara mumbled. "You better do something."

Kayla was sitting outside the bank watching the whole thing unfold. She started getting nervous once she saw the first police car pull up. Her first instinct was to get the fuck out of there, but she wasn't leaving her sister. She decided to wait it out and see what happened.

"There has to be a mistake. We don't know anything about this," Tamara pleaded as the officers approached her and Tiffany. They had serious looks on their faces.

"Ma'am, place your hands behind your back."

"Officer, there's been some kind of mix-up," Tiffany tried explaining. "If you give me a minute to call the lady that sent them to us, I promise she will tell you we didn't steal them."

"Lord, please don't let them take me to jail," Tamara began praying as she was also placed in cuffs.

The officers escorted them over to the lobby. "Take a seat," the lead officer instructed. He whipped out his writing pad and then walked over to the tellers to get their statements. Tiffany was hoping Kayla would walk through the door and save their asses, but when the lobby doors chirped again, Tiffany realized they were definitely going to jail.

Rico had the nastiest scowl on his face as he bypassed Tiffany and Tamara and walked straight over to the teller area where the officers were standing. Tamara remembered the man from the time she hid in the dressing room. He was the one her mother was having sex with.

"We are so screwed!" Tiffany said.

Rico, the tellers, and the officers headed back in the girls' direction. Tamara tried to hide the fear. All this to save a boy that probably didn't want to be with her, and that she felt obligated to help.

"Sir, do you know these two individuals?" the officer asked.

They could see the fire burning in his eyes as he darted them from one of them to the other. His brows furrowed and

his nose flared as it always did when he was angry.

"Yes, Officer, I know them both. This one has a sister that works for me, and this one," he said, pointing at Tamara, "her mother works for me."

"It's up to you if you want to press charges, sir. We can take them down and get them processed for two counts of check fraud so that this doesn't happen again."

Rico continued to look at the two girls wondering if Kayla and Akira had anything to do with all of this. He could tell that they were scared shitless. Tamara had tears coming down her face as she stared at him with pleading eyes.

"Can you excuse us for a moment, please?" Rico said to the officers. They stepped back giving him some space. "Those tears don't work with me. Why were you trying to steal my money, and before you answer, remember that this won't end well for either of you if you lie to me."

They both knew what that last statement meant, and fear really set in at that moment. Tamara told him about Ed's situation, hoping he wouldn't let them go to jail.

"Please don't let them take us to jail," Tiffany said to Rico.

"You both are going to work for me to pay off all the money I'm missing out on by being here. Once you do that, I will help you get him out. Are we clear on that?"

They both looked at each other and then at him, nodding in agreement. Anything not to go to jail. They were wondering what they would be doing.

"Meet me at my club at five o'clock tonight, and don't be late. I don't want to ever see either of you again," Rico said. He turned to the officers. "I don't want to press charges this time."

Tamara exhaled a sigh of relief. She was happy they weren't going to jail, but still was wondering how she would help Ed.

"As you wish, sir," the officer said, taking the cuffs off the girls.

"Thank you for calling," Rico said, winking at the teller.

"No problem! If you would, follow me to my office so I can make some notations and freeze all your accounts until we can get them closed out and new ones opened."

Tamara and Tiffany waited until the police and Rico were out of sight, then hauled ass out the door, walking fast as they could toward the car. Kayla quickly pulled out into traffic, trying to get away from the bank. Tamara was upset she didn't get the money.

"What the fuck happened in there? Don't leave anything out," Kayla said heading home, glad they made it out.

FOURTEEN

Rico entered the bank manager's office and closed the door. She was leaning on her desk smiling at him, when he pulled out a thick envelope and gave it to her. It was full of cash. The sight of all the money excited her, and the fact that it was hers this time made her pussy wet.

"Thank you for contacting me about that situation. Were you able to wash the other money for me yet?"

"I'm working on it, but what will I get out of it?"

"What do you want? We never had the chance to talk about that yet," he said, sitting down in the chair in front of her desk.

Rico's bosses had made a deal with her to wash some of the drug money they had sitting around. The bank they were using before had become a liability, and the manager had to be put to sleep, permanently.

"I told you to let your bosses make me a deal I can't resist. In the meantime though, you can do something for me," she stated, scooting back onto the edge of her desk. "I want you to fuck me right here."

She uncrossed her legs, leaving them open as she sat on the desk. Rico looked right up under her short skirt, to her pussy. She wasn't wearing any panties, which gave him an unobstructed view of her puffy lips.

"Really?" was all he could manage to say.

"Really," she replied. "Make sure the door is locked."

Rico jumped at the chance to try out some new snatch. He checked the door and turned around to see the bank manager hiking her skirt up to her waist. Rico bricked up at the sight of it. He knelt down in front of her, lining his face directly up with her pussy, ready to suck on her clit. He pushed the back of her thighs up, spreading them as wide as they could go. Her asshole came into view below the pink slit of her pussy lips.

"Let me test your head game out," she moaned excitedly.

"You want some of this good head, huh?" he teased, flicking at her clit.

"Yes!"

He speared his tongue into her pussy's opening, then lapped up toward her clit. The bank manager was using her fingertips to massage her pussy as he sucked on her clit a little, then went back down to her ass. His tongue was just inches away from where he wanted to stick it. Going for her asshole was risky, but he needed to find out.

With his hands still holding up her thighs from underneath, he used his thumbs to spread her butt cheeks. In one smooth motion, he glided the tip of his tongue down from her pussy slit, across the narrow bridge of smooth skin that separated her holes, and around the rim of her asshole.

"Mmmmmm," she moaned, wiggling her butt on the

desk. "You know how to make a girl feel good, don't you?"

"You ain't seen nothing yet," Rico answered.

He made his tongue into a stiff rod, then slowly pushed it inside the smooth, pink muscle of her asshole. She was hot and spicy inside. He glided in and out, feeling her ass clutch at his tongue like an eager little mouth. Her body seemed to go limp with pleasure. She rolled sideways on the desk until she was lying on her stomach and her feet were resting on the floor. That gave him even better access to her asshole. He held her ass open and licked up and down her crack, making it shine.

"We have to fuck real quick, because I have to be somewhere," he said, checking his phone. "You gonna let me test that ass?"

"Mmmmm, yes, just be gentle please, and use a condom," she said. She was massaging her glistening hole with a finger, as if she couldn't stand to be neglected now that his tongue wasn't in it. "This feels so good."

Rico slipped out a condom from his pocket, tore open the package, and quickly rolled the rubber down the length of his erection. He slid inside her pussy, pumping ferociously. Once his dick was wet enough, he pulled out. He pressed the head of his dick against her asshole, then pushed his hard dick inside. She gasped for air as he continued pushing.

"Oh shit, yes," she yelled out, clenching her ass together.

When he was all the way in, he held his position for a

few seconds. She gave a long, deep groan as they both savored the moment. Then it was time to make her cum. He moved slowly at first, then sped up the pace. She rubbed her clit while he ripped her asshole wide open.

"You like that, don't you?" Rico asked between pumps.

"Oh God, yes, give it to me, baby," she said, almost weeping with pleasure.

Rico pulled out of her ass, removed the condom, then inserted his dick into her soaking wet pussy. As he pumped away, he reached around, grabbing her breasts. The squeezing of her nipples sent her over the edge. She cried out with a trembling climax. Her pussy spasmed around his dick with such a force that it practically milked out an orgasm from him. He clenched his teeth and grunted as released his cum.

"So when can I expect you to have that money washed and into my new account?" he asked, holding himself inside her.

"By the end of the day," she replied, catching her breath. He smacked her on the ass, then pulled out.

She hurried up and fixed her clothes, grabbing some tissue to wipe herself. When Rico fixed his clothes and walked out the office, all eyes were on him. The other tellers were smiling from ear to ear as they continued tending to their customers. Rico threw his shades on and walked out of the bank with a smile on his face.

FIFTEEN

"Are you okay in there?"

"Yeah, I'm good. I just want to get the hell out of here," Ed responded.

He was being held in Curran-Fromhold Correctional Facility, on State Road. Even though his cousin's girl was making sure he had money on his books, he still felt like he had nothing. Out of all the drugs he had sold, this was his first time ever getting arrested. They had charged him as an adult, even though he was only seventeen, due to the severity of the crime.

"I'm going to do what I have to do to get you out of there, okay?" Tamara said, feeling like she was about to cry.

"I have someone working on a lawyer for me. I can sit this out," he lied. He didn't want her thinking he wasn't strong enough to do time.

"You have one minute remaining on this call," the operator said, interrupting their conversation.

"Look, I have to go, but I will call you tomorrow, okay?" Ed stated.

After Tamara pressed end on her phone, she started to cry, wondering would her life ever be the same. She wished she would have never dressed sexy that night, and Ed would still be home. It was that moment that she decided to do what

she had to in order to help her friend.

~ ~ ~

Ed sat on the block watching *Claws*, when the CO called him to the desk. He waited until the show went to commercial before seeing what she wanted.

"Mr. Jones, you are wanted across the hall in the lieutenant's office," she stated, giving him a pass.

"What they want me for? I didn't do shit," Ed replied with an attitude.

"I don't know, sir. I got a call to send you over, and that's what I do," she told him. "Now catch the door before it closes."

Another inmate held the door for him, as he was coming back from medical. Ed walked over to the lieutenant's office and knocked on the door. When he walked in, Officer Mason was standing there.

"Ed, Kayla is your cousin, right?" she asked, standing there.

"Yeah, why?"

"Okay, I was just making sure I had the right person. She told me to look out for you while you're here. Are you cool with your cellmate?"

"He's alright," Ed said, wondering what this was all about. "We bust it up sometimes, but that's about it."

"Do you trust him?"

"I don't know yet, but so far he has never given me a reason not to."

"I'm working a double tonight. I put the both of you on work detail, so your door will be open all night. I'm going to come see you later, so make sure you're awake." She signed his pass, then sent him back to the block.

When he returned to his block, he was still thinking about what she said. He wondered what she could possibly be bringing him. Then it all made sense. She was going to drop some dope off to him. He got really excited with that thought.

"Yo, celly, let me holler at you real quick," he said, heading to his cell.

"What's up?"

"Yo, our door is gonna be open tonight because I have to make a move. I need to know if you rocking with me or not," Ed said.

"I'm here for murking a nigga, so count me in," lil Dev said boldly.

"No, it's nothing like that. I'm on another level, bro. I just wanted to make sure we were on the same page. We'll find out tonight, but roll out so I can use the bathroom."

After his celly left, Ed put the curtain up. As he relieved himself, he thought about all the money he was going to make in there. He couldn't wait until tonight.

~ ~ ~

It was after midnight when their cell popped open. Ed sat up on his bunk and then threw on his shoes. When he walked to the door, he could see officer Tinsley heading toward his cell. She opened the door and walked in. Lil Dev sat up when he smelled her perfume.

"Hey, guys! Your cousin must really love you. She knows how I get down for that money."

"So what do you have for me?" Ed asked, rubbing his hands together anxiously. "You had me hyped up all day."

"I had to wait until Kayla paid me. That's why I said tonight," she replied, closing the cell door, but not locking it.

When she started to unbutton her uniform, Ed thought she was hiding the work on her. He was even more excited when she revealed her firm breasts.

"How much did she send me?"

"Huh?" Catrena said with a confused look on her face. "What you mean how much did she send you? I know you didn't think I was smuggling drugs in here."

She started to button her shirt back up. Ed realized she wasn't there to bring him drugs. At that moment, he felt like a nut.

"Whoa, ma, my bad. I misunderstood what was going on. Don't leave!" he said, grabbing her hand. "Entertain me and

my celly."

Catrena started taking her clothes off as lil Dev jumped off his bunk and sat on the stool to get a better view of the fine-ass CO in their cell. Ed's dick immediately rose to the occasion once she started removing her pants. She walked over to where Ed was sitting, then sat down next to him.

"You sit there and watch," she said to lil Dev. Ed winked at him, letting him know to chill for a second. "Come here!"

They embraced and kissed openmouthed, and Ed started fondling her titties. Catrena stood up, and Ed helped her out of her panties and bra. She stood naked before them. Lil Dev also had a growing erection now.

"Lay on my bunk," Ed said.

She did as she was told, spreading her legs. Ed buried his face in her vagina, his tongue licking the full length of her clit. She rotated her ass and held his head firmly against her pussy as she energetically fucked his face. He moved up to her swollen nipples, which stood out firmly from the rest of her body. He pulled and tweaked them until it made her squeal in delight.

"Why don't both of you hurry up and remove your clothes. There isn't much time."

They both quickly removed their clothes, not caring that they were standing there naked in front of each other. Catrena was shocked how big Ed's dick was. She thought it was every bit of ten inches, and lil Dev's wasn't far behind.

She felt like she was in heaven as she took the head of Ed's dick into her mouth, sucking it furiously. Her head bobbed up and down in rhythm with his movement.

"That's right, suck this dick!" he moaned.

Catrena moaned as he pushed her head further down on his dick, causing her to gag a little. He closed his eyes, enjoying the sensation. After sucking him off for awhile, she pulled out and began licking the full length of his shaft, along with his balls.

"Fuck me," she said, leaning over on the table.

Ed positioned his dick in line with her dripping pussy. Her ass rose high in the air, exposing both her puckered brown asshole and her swollen pussy lips. Ed placed the head inside, then filled her hot hole to the limit. Moans of pleasure escaped from Catrena's lips.

"Oh yes, fuck me hard. Fuck my hot pussy. Oh yes, yes!"

Catrena grabbed lil Dev's dick and jammed it into her mouth. It caught him by surprise but felt oh so good. Ed was giving her a full pounding from the back while lil Dev gave her a mouthful from the front.

"Aghhhh," Ed yelled, finally letting out a moan, releasing inside her. Cum leaked from her pussy and dripped down her leg when he pulled out. "Damn, I needed that."

She stood up and sat on the desk, giving lil Dev a view of her still leaking pussy. She used two fingers to spread her lips, then pulled lil Dev inside. While he plowed away at her

pussy, she gave Ed a look as if she wanted some more of him instead of his cellmate. When lil Dev finally shot his load, she used one of their washcloths to wash up. Then she put her uniform back on.

"Tell my cousin I said thank you," Ed said, catching his breath. "We definitely have to do this again soon if you're up to it."

"As long as y'all keep your mouth shut and that money is right, we can definitely do it again. Like my bitches say, money makes me cum, along with a hard dick," she smirked.

"Well just tell my cousin that I said to handle her business and everything will be cool."

"Will do! Don't forget to sweep and mop the day room before you go to sleep. I'll be back later to check, and it better be done," she stated before walking out of the cell.

"Damn, celly, you need to put me on the team if I beat this case. You got connections," lil Dev said as they headed out to clean up.

Ed didn't respond because he was still shocked himself. They just partied a correctional officer on his bunk. It didn't get no better than that, he thought.

SIXTEEN

Akira was trying to figure out how to alleviate a problem that had suddenly resurfaced. She thought she had left it in her past, but somehow old habits are hard to get rid of. She was in the kitchen fixing dinner for her kids before she went to work. She noticed a change in Tamara, and wondered what brought it on. She was starting to dress like a young lady and went out more with her friend Tiffany. What really stuck out to her was every time she received a certain call, she would run either outside or into her room. Akira knew it meant only one thing. She had a boyfriend and was trying to keep it a secret.

"Kayla, I have some shit to take care of, so I won't be home until later on tonight," Jeff said when he walked into the kitchen.

"So who's gonna watch DJ? I have to work," she replied.

"Tamara can watch her brother. She don't have shit to do!"

"She has something to do, Jeff. She deserves to have a life too," Akira shot back. She was starting to get an attitude. "Me and Tamara didn't have this baby, me and you did. She's going out with her friends, so you will just have to take him with you."

"Well this is very important, and I have to handle this,

baby. It will benefit all of us. Akira, when you met me, you knew how I got down," he began. "Now you said I have to start providing for this family, so let me do me."

Akira already knew what that meant. Jeff used to do dirty work for people that couldn't do it themselves. In other words, he was a murderer for hire. When she first met him, he was running away from a shooting at the club. The shooting had been over her. One of the customers tried to rob her as she was heading to her car after work. Jeff was coming out the door when it happened, and intervened. They ended up getting together, and he promised her that he would leave that life behind him. Up until now, he had kept his word.

"I'll take care of my son like I always do," Akira said, giving up. She knew she couldn't change him even if she tried. She had to let him be the man he was.

"Don't be like that, Akira. I'm going to have something special for you when I get back okay," he said, walking up behind her.

He stuck his hand inside her sweatpants and started playing with her pussy. He always knew how to turn her on, but right now wasn't the time. She needed to get to work.

"Mmmmm, that feels nice, but I have to finish making this chicken," she said, pulling his hand out of her pants.

"I'll see you later." His phone rang, indicating that he had a text message. He left her standing there with a wet pussy. She would take care of that problem later when she

counted all the money she made tonight.

Akira hated that Gene had threatened to cause trouble on her job if she came to the club. Instead of going back to work, she made up a story to take a few days off. She was tired of hiding and decided to face her problems head on. She still never told Jeff that Tamara's father was in town.

Earlier today she had met up with Rico and told him about the situation. He promised her that he wouldn't let anyone hurt her, especially while in his club. Akira told Tamara that she had to watch her brother because Jeff had to leave. At first Tamara protested to no avail, but then a plan popped in her head. She called Tiffany up and asked if she could watch DJ while she took care of something.

~ ~ ~

The black SUV pulled up in front of where Tamara was standing. She was told to walk a couple of blocks away from her house so she wouldn't be seen. The back passenger window came down slowly.

"Get in," the occupant said. Tamara looked around before opening the door and getting inside.

"Why did you want to see me?" she asked.

"We have some unfinished business to discuss. You and your friend tried to steal money from me, and I would like to know where you got the checks from."

"I didn't steal them from you," Tamara replied, starting to get a little nervous.

"Well maybe I should ask your mother if she did it," he stated, pulling out his cell phone.

"Okay, okay! It wasn't my mother that gave them to me," she blurted out. "I got them from Kayla so I could help my friend."

"I knew it was her. I just needed to be sure first. Your mother is as loyal as they come. She is probably the only one I trust in that whole club. Even my managers are untrustworthy and need to be watched," he said, showing her his phone. It was a live video feed of his club. He had a direct link to every camera in the building. "Pull over right here."

They pulled in front of Melrose Diner on 15th & Snyder Ave. Rico was well known in the place, because everyone he walked past spoke to him as the waitress escorted them to their seats. Once they were both seated, he questioned Tamara some more to see if he could break her. She told him the whole story about the day in question.

Rico studied her face as she talked, looking for signs of deception. As he stared at her, he also noticed how beautiful she was. This was a totally different young lady than the one he caught peeking at him and her mother. She had on tight jeans and a fitted shirt that exploited her whole body. Rico couldn't keep his eyes off her.

"They are ready for you now," the sexy waitress said.

"Come with me. I want to show you something," he said, taking her by the hand, leading her toward the back of the restaurant.

They walked through a few doors, and it was like they stepped into a whole new world. There were a bunch of men sitting at a round table. Rico motioned for Tamara to have a seat while he took care of business. At the table were some very powerful people she had never seen before.

"Let's get down to business," Merv stated, signaling for the ladies holding the duffle bags in their hands to step forward.

They started dumping the contents out onto the table. Tamara had never seen so much money in her life. There were piles and piles of cash sitting there. No one even noticed that she was in the room, because they were so focused on the money and what they were there for. Tamara was still wondering why she was there. About thirty-five minutes later, her questions were answered.

"She will be working in one of my massage parlors," Rico said, pointing to Tamara. "So all I want y'all to do is focus on the collections."

"Who is she?" Merv asked, staring at Tamara. Butterflies ran all through Tamara's stomach, as all eyes were now on her.

"That's my new investment. We had a misunderstanding, but she will be working it off."

"She's your responsibility if anything goes wrong. Well if that's all, I have other affairs that need my attending to. This meeting is adjourned," Herb chimed in.

Everyone stood up from the table and left the room while the girls started placing the money on the table through the counting machines. Instead of Tamara being mad that she was being put to work in some massage parlor, she was fascinated by Rico's leadership. At the same time though, she was scared of what could happen to her if her mom found out what she'd done or what she was about to be doing.

When Rico finished up, they ate, and then he took her back home. He parked at the end of her block so they could talk. Rico got straight to the point, not sugarcoating anything.

"Your friend Tiffany has been working in my spot for about two months now. Her peoples have no idea what she's doing, and I will keep your involvement a secret also," he said, making sure he had her full attention before continuing. "Nobody steals from me and just walks away without any consequences."

"What all do I have to do, Rico?" Tamara asked, scared.

"You will be giving men and women special massages. You don't have to do anything you don't want to, okay? I can tell you this much though, the more you do, the more money you'll make," he stated.

Tamara knew exactly what he was talking about, and that

made her paranoid. She had never had sex before, except when she was raped. Those college boys took her precious virginity, and she never had the chance to actually have sex willingly yet. She wished Ed was home so she could experience it, but that wasn't going to happen right now. She had talked to him earlier and found out that it may be a year before he even got a trial.

"Do I have to do this?"

"Either that or I put your ass on the corner," he said seriously. At that moment, Tamara realized she had made a big mistake. "It's your choice, baby, so what's it gonna be?"

"You said I don't have to do anything, right?"

Rico shook his head.

"Okay, but how long do I have to do this?"

"Until I feel as though your debt is paid. You will report to work with Tiffany tomorrow morning. If your mother asks any questions, just say you found a summer job. I'll talk to you later." He leaned over and gave her a kiss on the cheek. When Tamara stepped out of the SUV. Rico rolled the window down. "Oh, and Tamara, you have a body like your mom. You need to use it wisely." He pulled off, leaving her with something to think about.

~ ~ ~

"Why didn't you tell me you were working at some

massage parlor?" Tamara snapped at her friend as soon as she walked in.

"I didn't know I had to answer to you, Mom," Tiffany responded sarcastically.

"I'm serious, Tiff. He's making me work there with you starting tomorrow. I wish we never tried to cash those checks. We can't let my mom find out about what we're doing, and you can't tell Kayla either, okay?"

Tiff nodded.

"So show me what I have to do!"

"Girl, it will be fun, I'm telling you. You will make so much money, and then you can buy whatever you want," she said excitedly. "Just follow my lead and you'll be okay. Did you talk to Ed?"

"Earlier today."

"Well I'm going home. The car will pick us up around twelve, so be at my crib early so we can get ready. Your brother is in his room taking a nap."

"Thank you for watching him."

"Anything for you, girl. We're stuck with each other now," she said, walking out the door.

After Tiffany left, Tamara took a quick shower, then lay across her bed naked. She couldn't stop thinking about all the money that had been on the table. She even wondered what Rico had those women doing. Usually Ed would be on her mind when she was lying in bed, but for some reason her

thoughts were on Rico. She could still smell his scent, and it had her wet. She found him very sexy, and was starting to forget all about Ed.

SEVENTEEN

Kayla and Akira were onstage doing their act while the crowd was in a frenzy. They were eating each other's pussy as money flew from every direction. They both came simultaneously, causing the crowd to erupt with cheering. Akira grabbed the money and then headed into the back. Kayla came in a few minutes later so they could split their proceeds.

"Girl, you have my pussy on fire," Kayla said.

"Shit, mine too! I'm going to fuck the shit out of one of these niggas out there tonight. Then I'm going to go home and give my man some."

"I hear that." Kayla smiled.

She wiped off and then headed out onto the floor to mingle. The place was rocking tonight because there was a special guest in the building. Fetty Wap was in the VIP section, popping bottles with about six dancers. His entourage was about twenty strong, and they were all fucked up off the loud.

"Everyone make some fucking noise for my man Fetty Wap up in this motherfucker," the DJ announced. The spotlight shined on him and his crew.

Akira was making her way toward their section, when out of the corner of her eye, there he was, watching her. Gene

was sitting in a booth, drinking a bottle of liquor. She could tell he was here to start some shit. She quickly ran to the dressing room to retrieve her phone. She texted Jeff letting him know there was a problem at work.

"Bitch, didn't I tell you not to come to this fucking club again?"

She turned around, and Gene was standing in the doorway. When he was close enough, she noticed his pupils were so dilated that you could barely see his iris. Akira knew that look could only mean trouble.

"You can't be in here. Gene, you have to leave," she told him.

"Bitch, don't tell me what the fuck to do." He smacked the shit out of Akira, causing her to grab her face. "Grab your shit. It's time to get out of here."

Akira tried to find something to hit him with. He approached her again, ready to swing, when security rushed in to help her. They grabbed him and forcefully removed him from the room.

"Bitch, I'm going to fuck you up when I catch you."

Akira wasn't scared, because she knew Jeff was on his way, and he didn't play when it came to her. After he was escorted out by security, Akira did another act with Kayla before getting dressed to leave. She didn't know what was taking Jeff so long to get there, so she decided it was time to leave. After calling him a few times with no answer, she

asked security to walk her to the car, to make sure she was safe.

As she drove down Columbus Avenue, she never noticed the dark-colored car following her. When she stopped at a red light, it pulled alongside her. Before she could even react, the driver had the window down and a gun pointed directly at her.

Pop! Pop! Pop!

The shots shattered the window, and broken glass splashed her in the face. She tried to duck, but it was too late as three more shots rang out, hitting her in the head and chest area. The driver in the dark car sped off before anyone could see had shot her.

~ ~ ~

The next day Tamara hadn't heard from her mother. It was typical of Akira to do that, so Tamara wasn't worried. Anytime that happened, it was because she had to work late and decided to stay at Kayla's house. Tamara let Jeff know she was leaving for work and to keep an eye on his son, then headed over to Tiffany's. After they finished getting ready, they headed outside to the awaiting SUV.

Tiffany and Tamara were the first girls to arrive at the massage parlor. When the doors opened, the first client came walking in. Coincidentally he came in asking for two girls.

Not even a minute at her new job, and Tamara had to work already. This was her first appointment, and she was nervous.

The middle-aged Caucasian stood there with a smile on his face. He had the weirdest request that anyone could ever imagine. They took him into a room, where he stripped down naked, and lay on the table in a fetal position. He nodded his head up and down, giving them the signal. Tamara, who was completely new to this, waited for her friend to take the lead. Tiffany could sense her friend's hesitation.

"Just follow me and we'll get this over with quick."

Tiffany pulled her blouse over her head, then popped her bra loose, releasing her breasts. Her areolas looked like huge chocolate cookies, and her nipples were so tiny like Hershey Kisses. Tamara and the man stared at them in amazement. Looking at her friend's breasts made Tamara second-guess her own. She had a gorgeous body, but Tiffany's was flawless.

She slowly followed Tiffany's lead, and removed her shirt, introducing her cups to the room. The man looked up at them as they stood there topless at his request. Right in front of his face he had the best of both worlds, and loved it. The man closed his eyes with anticipation on his face.

"What do we do next?" Tamara whispered to Tiff.

"I'll show you," she replied.

Tiffany stood in front of him, and with no warning she

began tickling the man's midsection. He giggled and squirmed like a kid. When he looked up at Tamara, who was watching in disbelief, the look in his eyes scared her into joining in. She understood that she better get to work, being that he had paid them three hundred dollars apiece for a tickle orgy, as he called it. Tamara was hesitant at first, but once she found a spot, it became quite easy. The two of them worked like the perfect tag team.

"No, no! Stop!" the man laughed, not really wanting them to stop. "Oh no!" he giggled as he turned over.

Tamara tickled his midsection while Tiffany worked on his feet. The man started moving all over the table with enjoyment. The girls were laughing at the way he reacted.

After a while, it started to become quite entertaining to Tamara, and she forgot how weird it actually was. She tickled him like she tickled her little brother, totally forgetting he was a grown-ass man, who was paying for it. He started shaking really bad, and then suddenly, without warning, he started squirting like a garden hose.

"No, no, no!" he screamed, trying to control himself, but couldn't.

His hot lava shot everywhere. Tiffany managed to get out of the way in the nick of time, but Tamara wasn't so lucky. Some of his gooey sperm landed on her neck, disgusting her to no end.

"What the fuck?" she snapped as she stared at the man

lying there, mouth wide open with shame.

She grabbed her shirt, then stormed out the room before she totally lost it. Tiffany, who was all too familiar with him, just laughed because it had happened to her also.

EIGHTEEN

A few hours later, Tamara had cleaned up and was feeling better. She was starting to relax just a bit, but still was a little uneasy. She strutted down the long narrow hall with false confidence, trying hard to cover up her nervousness. She thought she wouldn't be able to handle the whole thing and was ready to leave, but Tiff begged her to stay because she didn't want anything bad to happen to her friend. She sat there all morning watching dudes flock into the building, two and three at a time. It felt like a club. Appointments were booked for every hour, not including the walk-ins.

A total of six girls, not including Tamara, were working. Of the seven, she was the rookie to the business. She only serviced the one customer she and Tiff had done together. There were two drop-dead-gorgeous Latin girls, an exotic looking Filipino girl, a classy looking white chick, and one picture-perfect black girl, besides her and her friend. The only thing the other women had in common with each other was the extensive body enhancement work that they'd had done, which gave them an advantage over Tiffany and Tamara.

Tamara's high self-esteem was being questioned. She was beginning to like her body, but with all the customers passing her by, she thought she wasn't their type. Just as she

started second-guessing herself, Rico came strolling through the doors, staring at her.

"Why aren't you working?" he asked.

"I don't have a customer yet," she replied, staring at him.

"Now you do!" he said, pointing to himself.

Tamara thought it would be easier to digest, until her time came. Now she was ready to run out the door. As she stood at the door to the room, she realized there was no turning back. She looked over her shoulder at Rico, whose eyes were glued to her butt. They stepped into the room, and she closed the door. The room had the same setup as a legitimate massage parlor.

Tamara stared him up and down, noticing how attractive he really was. Everything about him screamed money. From the iced-out Rolex and flawless jewelry, to his clothes and footwear. She could see why her mom cheated on Jeff. It made her feel uncomfortable, knowing how she was feeling being near him. Deep down she wished he was hers. In a perfect world, he probably would be, but she knew this world was in no way perfect.

He quickly took the lead of the situation by pulling his shirt off. His muscular physique was of a man who was fresh out of the gym. He pulled his pants off and stood only in his boxers. The erection he already had to her exactly what was on his mind. The last time she saw it was at the club, and now she was getting another view up close and personal. She quickly looked away as he stood there with no shame,

wanting her to see it.

"What's good, baby girl? I ain't with the small talk and bullshit. I let my money do the talking for me," he said, digging into his pocket.

He pulled out a big-ass knot of money and began flicking through the bills. The sight of the money damn near made her mouth water, but she hid her thirst.

"What would you like to do?" she asked nervously.

"Like I told you before, ain't no money in massages, so you figure out what I want," he said boldly. She stood there dumbfounded. "I want some of that pussy."

"Rico, you know I don't want to do that. We talked about this already," she said. His bluntness caught her by surprise.

"I know you're new around here, but you need to get with the program, and fast. These niggas only come here for one thing. The money is in that pussy," he said, pointing between her legs.

Tamara was stunned. She wished he wouldn't act like that. Any other woman would feel disrespected at the way he was talking, but it turned her on. She wasn't telling him that though.

"Well you're gonna have to get some other girl," she said, walking toward the door.

"Okay, okay, hold up. I'll take the massage."

Tamara turned around, not sure if she wanted to or not.

"Come on, but just remember that you and your friend might be paying me back for a long time," he said, still

letting her know he was in charge.

Rico peeled off his boxers, then stood there naked with nothing except his socks and jewelry on. She tried hard to keep her eyes off his dick. He walked over to the massage table and lay flat on his stomach. Tamara walked over and stood at the table with uncertainty on her face. She had never given a professional massage in her life. This was her boss, so she was going to try like hell. She thought he was testing her, and wondered if he did this to the other girls as well, or if she was the first. Nervously she grabbed both of his shoulders and gripped them tightly.

"Ah-ah," he said, disapprovingly. She looked at him wondering what she was doing wrong. He pointed to her breasts while staring into her eyes.

"What, you want topless?" she asked, remembering what Tiffany had told her about what the customers would ask for. "That will be one fifty."

"Nah, I ain't no tittie man. I wanna see what's in those jeans," he said with a smile.

Tamara swallowed the lump of nervousness in her throat before she pulled her shirt over her head. She slowly fumbled with the latch on the back of her bra before it opened, releasing her perky breasts. She unzipped her jeans, and the sight of her hairless pussy peaking over the zipper blew his mind. She wasn't wearing any panties, thanks to Tiffany's advice.

Rico examined her beautiful, tight body in complete awe.

Tamara noticed the look in his eyes, and it built her confidence. She was now standing there boldly and confidently.

"That will be two fifty," she said, holding her hand out patiently.

"Damn, I don't get an employee discount?" he joked. He reached over for his pants lying on the floor, and dug into his pocket. He pulled the money out and counted it.

"Nope," she said, smiling.

He gave her a seductive look that weakened her legs. He held the money in his hand, attempting to taunt her with it first.

"Turn around first and let me see it," he demanded.

She snatched the money out of his hand, then turned around slowly and seductively. Rico's eyes bulged out of his head once he saw the size of her ass. He had totally underestimated her body. What looked like the perfect little onion in those jeans was really the size of a beach ball in the nude.

"Now what do you want me to do? Do you want me to make it clap?" she asked. She had seen her mother performing this act plenty of times, and now she was doing it.

She had been practicing in the mirror; that's why she was good at it. She looked over her shoulder at Rico, and saw that he was mesmerized. He couldn't even speak. He just nodded his head up and down in a trance-like state. Tamara jumped

off the floor a few inches, and once she landed, her ass made a clapping noise. She kept doing it until his erection damn near smacked him in the face. Now she was the one who was mesmerized. She couldn't believe how big he was.

"Now turn on your stomach please."

Rico flipped over at her command. Tamara started working on his shoulders the best way she knew how. The massage was quite bland, boring the shit out of Rico. After a few minutes of torture, he could no longer take it. He looked up at her, square in her eyes.

"That is not how you give a massage. I can see why you haven't had any customers," he said as he got up off the table. "You lay down. I'm gonna show you how to do it the right way."

Tamara stood there with a puzzled look on her face. He was the boss, so she crawled on the table. Rico didn't hesitate to start massaging her shoulders. His hands were like that of a trained masseuse, as he dug into her shoulders, trying to work out the kinks. Once she was relaxed, he climbed onto the table, straddling himself over her back thighs.

His testicles rested on the back of her thighs, making her pussy moisten. Her cheeks stared up at him, causing his mouth to water. He kept his eyes glued on it as he worked his way down her arms, massaging them with his thumbs.

"How does that feel?" he asked. "Good, don't it?"

"Yes," was all she could get out through her deep

breathing.

Rico skipped over her hands, jumping straight to her waistline. He dug his thumbs deep into her skin while his fingers caressed her sides. When he hit her spot, she jumped. She moaned softly before her body tensed up. He continued on until she became at ease again. He slid up, allowing his manhood to slide in between her cheeks.

Tamara had a flashback to when she was being raped, and jumped again, but he had her pinned so she couldn't move. When she opened her eyes, she realized that she was with Rico. Her body totally relaxed all of a sudden. He gripped her cheeks, spreading them wide as he massaged away.

"Mmmmm," she let out a soft moan, then closed her eyes.

Tamara could feel her juices starting to leak from her love box and onto the sheet. She arched her back, enjoying the massage. Rico leaned over, his chest resting on her back. He placed his lips against her earlobe and whispered into her ear.

"Let me stick just the head in. I got $500 dollars for you right now, okay?"

Tamara snapped out of her horny spell and thought about Ed and who she wanted her real first time to be with. Ed was going to be gone for a long time, and Rico was here in the flesh showing her so much attention. She sighed a horny sigh. Her body was going through a change, and she wanted

so badly to experience this.

"Damn," she said under her breath.

Rico realized he was giving her too much time to think, and he intensified the massage. He added a little grinding on her ass, and licked her earlobe.

"Is it okay?" he asked again.

Tamara couldn't believe she was feeling this way. "I don't know," she moaned. Her mouth said she didn't know, but her pussy was saying something totally different. She was ready to experience some good loving like the movies she had been watching.

"Can I put just the head in?" he asked again, this time grinding deeper into her butt.

After thinking about this man fucking her mom, and then the fact that he had her working in a massage parlor, Tamara made the only decision that felt right to her at that moment. She nodded her head up and down. With all the holding out she had been doing, she couldn't hold out any longer. Her pussy was yearning to be touched. "Please be gentle," she pleaded, grinding back.

"I got you, baby. Just relax."

NINETEEN

Someone was banging on the door while Jeff sat on the toilet. He hurried up and wiped himself, then pulled up his boxers to answer the door. Two plainclothes detectives stood there flashing their credentials.

"Are the relatives of Akira Moses here?" the female detective said, looking at Jeff standing there in his boxers.

"What is this in regard to?"

"There's been an accident, and she was shot. She's at Presbyterian Hospital in critical condition right now. Would you like us to give you a ride to see her?"

"No, I'll get there myself," Jeff told them. "Is that all?"

"Do you know anyone that would want to hurt her?"

"No, I don't! Now if you would excuse me, I have to get to the hospital," Jeff said, shutting the door in their face.

He immediately called Tamara's phone while he got dressed and got DJ ready. Her phone went straight to voicemail. He dialed again.

"You know what to do, so do it at the beep, BEEP!"

He left another message as they headed to the hospital. He needed to find out who shot his girl, because they were going to pay with their lives.

~ ~ ~

Jeff, Tamara, Tiffany, Kayla, and DJ all sat in the waiting room, waiting for the doctor to give them an update on Akira's condition. Rico stayed outside in the car. Tamara had finally checked her voicemail, and when she heard the message, she immediately got Rico to drive them to the emergency room.

About two hours later, the doctor came out and informed them they could go in and see her briefly. Tamara was the first to jump up. She grabbed DJ's hand and they all walked up the hall to Akira's room.

Akira had all kinds of tubes up her nose. The doctors wanted to place her in a medically induced coma, but had decided to wait. Tamara held her hand tightly hoping she would squeeze back.

"Mom, if you can hear me, please wake up." Tamara sighed. To her surprise, Akira slowly opened her eyes. Tamara's tears were still flowing down her face, but this time they were tears of joy. "Hey, Mom, how are you feeling?"

She still wasn't able to speak at the moment. However, she did squeeze Tamara's hand. Everyone was feeling a sigh of relief as they gathered around the bed. The doctor came in followed by the two detectives from earlier. The lead detective walked over to Akira, carrying a pad and pen. She was only there for one reason, and that was to catch her

suspect. She really didn't care about Akira's well-being.

"I just want to ask you a couple of questions if you're up to it," she began. "Do you know who did this to you?"

Once Akira was able to adjust her eyes, she looked around the room at all the sad faces, except for one. She stared with fear in her eyes.

"Mommy, are you okay?" Tamara asked.

"Ms. Moses, who did this to you?" the detective asked once again.

Akira had a scared look on her face and could see someone smiling at her. It was the person who shot her, and she thought the killer was coming back to finish the job. She looked up at the detectives and was ready to answer their questions. Just as Akira was about to tell them who did this to her, she went into cardiac arrest.

"What's happening to her?" Tamara said hysterically.

"I need everybody to get out now, please," the doctor yelled, hitting the emergency button.

They all backed out of the room as they watched the horror unfold. Doctors and nurses from everywhere rushed into the room.

"She's crashing. Prepare to shock her," the doctor shouted. "Clear," he said, shocking her.

Beep! Beep! Beep! Beeeeeeeeeeeep!

"Do it again! Clear."

They tried shocking her again to bring her back to life,

but then she crashed once again. They turned the machine up, then shocked her again as the nurse performed CPR in an effort to save their patient.

"Mommy, noooooo," Tamara cried out in fear. DJ didn't know why his sister was crying. He just started crying with her, holding on to her leg tightly.

"It's gonna be alright, Tamara," Tiffany said, consoling her friend.

Jeff was standing there with a blank expression on his face. The room was packed with hospital personnel, trying to save Akira's life. The detectives stood off to the side in a deep conversation of their own. Kayla sat on the bench, talking to someone on the phone. More and more of Akira's friends were starting to pile into the hospital. They all waited, hoping she would pull through.

Rico was still sitting outside in his car, talking on the phone. He wasn't trying to be inside a hospital full of cops. He was on a conference call with Merv, and Herb.

"So what do you want me to do? We can't say for sure that it was them."

"Just hold off until I can get some more info," Herb replied. "Just keep me posted on that situation."

"Will do," Rico said, ending the call. He looked at the people going in and out of the emergency room, and banged his head on the steering wheel. "Fuck, fuck, fuck!"

TWENTY

It had been almost six months since Tamara's mother died. She took it kind of hard at first, but had to get over it quick for the sake of her little brother. She had been taking care of him for the most part. Jeff was never around, or he would show up late to watch his son, knowing she had to be at work. This was one of those days where he hadn't shown up yet. Tamara made several calls, trying to contact him, but he wouldn't answer, as if he knew what she wanted.

When Rico came to pick her up, she told him she wouldn't be able to work because she had to watch DJ. Usually Rico wouldn't get involved with family affairs, but this time was different. She was one of his best workers, and she made them a lot of money at the massage parlor. Tamara already had customers waiting there for her. He made a phone call and then told her to bring her brother with her as he opened the door for them.

The white Cadillac pulled into the Fresh Grocer parking lot. Two men occupied the front seats, and the head of a third man could be seen in the backseat. The driver, Jeff, hopped out when he saw Tamara and his son pull up. She could see the anger on his face as she zipped up her jacket to cover the outfit she was wearing to work.

"Come on, DJ," she said, opening the passenger-side

door.

"Sit tight. I got this one," Rico stated, pushing the driver-side door open.

He stepped out of the all-black Porsche Cayenne, and not once did he look in the direction of Jeff, who was standing near the front of his vehicle. Rico picked lil DJ up out of the car seat, closing the door behind him. They headed over to where Jeff was standing.

Jeff stood there in confusion for a second, paralyzed with anger. Finally he snapped out of his zone and stormed toward Rico with rage. He looked over at Tamara, who was staring at them. He was so infuriated that he could barely put his words together.

"Bitch!" he shouted. "Why are you bringing my son here while I'm taking care of shit? Who the fuck is this?"

He snatched DJ from Rico. Both the front and back passenger doors of the Cadillac opened up wildly. Rico stood there calm and cool as the men trotted toward them. They both stood there next to Jeff, waiting for something to pop off.

Rico stared into Jeff's eyes with a blank look on his face, without saying a word. Not once did he look at the two other men. The three of them were shocked by his courage, but charged it off as another prideful dude trying to impress a woman.

"Bitch, if you ever—" Jeff said, pointing to Tamara.

"If she ever what?" Rico asked, finally breaking his silence. A smirk spread across his face. "He's your son, not hers. She don't have to stay in the house watching him while you run the street."

The wicked look in his eyes caused the other two men concern, but Jeff was so angry that he didn't even notice. Rico stepped closer to him with determination, as if the other two men weren't even standing there. To all of their surprise, Rico stepped right up to Jeff's chest, staring into his eyes.

"That's the last bitch she gonna be."

"What, nigga? Who the fuck is you? That's my fucking stepdaughter, and my son. You don't have shit to do with this," he said, pointing to Tamara and DJ. "You're too fucking old to be around her anyway. She's only seventeen fucking years old."

Rico noticed the men sizing him up as if they were about to move on him. He wasn't bothered one bit by it. Tamara peeped something about to go down, and hopped out of the truck, with fear in her eyes.

"Rico," she whined. "Y'all don't," she pleaded to save him.

"I said that was the last bitch she gonna be. The next one, they gonna be scraping your ass off the asphalt," Rico said with coldness in his eyes, slightly lifting his shirt up exposing the handle of his Glock .40. The men backed away, surprised, but Rico stepped up further.

"Y'all get back in the truck. Y'all don't have nothing to do with this unless y'all put yourself in the middle of it," he said while gripping his gun. He then looked over to Tamara. "Get back in the truck."

"Okay!"

She didn't hesitate to follow his command. She walked over and got back in the truck, just as the two men were getting back into the Cadillac. There Jeff and Rico stood with only lil DJ in between them both. Jeff held his son close to him like a shield, in a cowardly manner.

"If you were home taking care of them, then I wouldn't have to. I got everything to do with that," he said as he pointed to Tamara. "That's my situation now, and you gone respect it. Don't let your feelings get you into something nobody will be able to get you out of. Whatever you do with your son is your business, but that right there is mine. Respect my situation, or me and you gonna have a situation. We clear on that?"

Jeff nodded his head up and down with his mouth wide open, not able to utter a word. He was far from a pussy, but today he was feeling like one. Rico knew he was wrong for fucking with a girl that was ten years younger than him, but he planned on molding her into a boss bitch. He saw the potential in her, and he would bring it to the light.

"This is our first meeting, and hopefully our last. You asked who I am. My name is Rico Chavez Jr. Now go do

your homework on me. I'm sure anybody you ask about me and tell about our little encounter will tell you that you're lucky it went this way," he said with a smile. "We can look at our meeting as an introduction and move forward, or we can take this into some gangsta shit."

He turned around and started walking back toward his truck. As he opened the driver's-side door, he looked up at Jeff. "The choice is yours. I'm with whatever." He got in his truck and pulled off, leaving Jeff there with something to think about.

TWENTY-ONE

Through some miracle, the judge lowered Ed's bail enough for the CO he had been fucking to persuade her parents to post his bail. He had sold her a dream of being with him. Now that he was out, he had to pay a special friend a visit. Tiffany had written him, letting him know that Tamara was messing with Rico now. That pissed him off, knowing he had gone to jail for protecting her ass. He felt as though she owed him loyalty, and since she said fuck him, he was going to use her ass to get what he wanted from Rico.

Ed pulled up to Kayla's crib and told the Uber driver to wait for him. He walked up to the door and knocked lightly. No answer. He asked the driver if he could use his phone, then called Tiffany.

"Where you at?"

"Who this?" Tiff asked, not recognizing the number.

"It's Ed! Are you home?"

"Yeah, where you at?"

"Open the door. I'm walking to your crib now." He ended the call, passed the driver back his phone, then headed over to Tiffany's crib.

She was standing in the door waiting for him. Her parents were out in Vegas celebrating their eighteen-year anniversary, so she had the house to herself. Ed walked in

and sat on the couch. Tiffany sat down next to him and told him the whole story of Rico and Tamara's relationship, hoping to gain his trust. She could tell he was intensely aware of her body being so close to his.

"There's no one here but us," she said, putting her hand on his shoulder, his body stirring to her touch.

"You're gonna help me get at her and that nigga," he said.

"Only if you fuck the shit out of me right now," she told him.

He knew he still had to go see Catrena when she got off work, or she would have a fit. Right now though, he had time to have a little fun. He reached over and unfastened Tiffany's shirt, and then grabbed her breasts. Tiffany gasped with enjoyment as he twiddled her nipples.

Ed started kissing her, sticking his tongue deep into her mouth. She started to rub his dick through the pants he was wearing. She sat on his lap, rubbing her pussy against his manhood. It made her panties get moist.

"I've masturbated thinking about the last time we fucked, plenty of times," she lied.

Tiffany stood up and slipped out of her shirt, then pulled him up with her and told him to suck on her titties, throwing her head back and emitting high, urgent gasps of pleasure as he tongued her down. He stuck his hand down her pants, tickling her clit. Her first orgasm hit like a bolt of lightning,

surging through her body. Ed clamped down on her nipples with his lips as she writhed beneath his touch.

"I want you to eat my pussy," she moaned.

Ed pulled her pants off, then pushed her down on the couch. He spread her thighs wide open and planted his face right in the center of her hairless and glistening pussy. First he eagerly licked her outer lips, making her cry out so loudly that it echoed throughout the building. Then he got right into her pussy hole. He lapped up her thick, delicious nectar as she ground against his tongue. She stuck a finger into her slit and swirled it around, moistening it thoroughly so she could taste her own juices.

"Come on, Ed," she screamed. "Get down on my clit and swallow it whole!"

At first his nose tickled tentatively at her swollen pearl, and then his mouth went crazy. He gave her the vacuum treatment, sucking so hard that she wanted it to go on forever. His hot tongue circled her clit over and over, making her cum again.

After a few minutes, Tiffany opened her legs even wider to give him all the access to her love tunnel. Her fingers dug deeply into his back muscles as another orgasm slammed through her body. His tongue game was on a hundred.

"Take your clothes off, baby. I want to feel you inside me right now," she stated, pulling at his button, trying to help him.

After getting his clothes off, he spread her legs, then entered her hot walls with his rock-hard penis. He gave her long, hard strokes, making her scream out in pleasure.

"Oh shit, yes, baby, you're hitting my spot."

She continued screaming out in ecstasy after each stroke from his massive erection. Ed was pumping so hard and fast that he didn't realize he was on the verge of ejaculating. Tiffany could feel all the buildup he had waited so long to release, and wanted to taste it.

"Fuck yeah, fuck me harder!" she groaned in his ear, encouraging him to give her his best.

"Oh God, I'm gonna cum," Ed rasped out. The tension in his body was unbearably good as he drove his dick into her again and again.

"Then fucking do it!" Tiffany wailed. He let out a loud moan, and she felt him shooting his hot sperm inside her soaked pussy. It was so hot and creamy, and it seemed to last forever. When he pulled out, Tiffany started sucking his dick, trying to empty the rest of it into her mouth.

"Now are you ready to help me get this bitch?"

"Whatever you need," she replied, exhausted from the sexcapade.

"Don't tell anyone I'm home. I want it to be a surprise," he said, rubbing her pussy, bringing her to another orgasm. She answered by sitting on his rising erection for another round, and Ed was more than happy to oblige.

TWENTY-TWO

Since the altercation, Tamara had been staying over at Rico's house until things cooled down. He had been teaching her how to drive so she could get around on her own. When she got off work, an all-white Honda Accord with pink trimmings was sitting in front of the building. Rico stood next to it, dangling the keys in the air. Tamara nearly lost her mind when she found out it was hers.

"Oh my God, thank you so much," she said, giving him a huge kiss.

"Look, be careful driving around with no license, okay? I have to take care of some things, so I'll see you at home later. If anything happens, just give me a call," he said, jumping in the car with his friend.

Tamara was so excited that she called Tiffany and told her the news. Tamara didn't pick up on the jealousy in her voice until she ended the call. Since she hadn't seen her baby brother in three days, she decided to pick him up from the daycare. She called Jeff and told him she was going to take him out to the mall and buy him something nice. She pulled up in front of the daycare and headed inside smiling, knowing he would be so glad to see her.

She walked into his classroom and then looked over to his assigned area with the hopes of his face brightening up

her day. She looked around in search of him, but he was nowhere to be found. The young aid ran over to her.

"Your father came to get him early today," she said, referring to Jeff.

"Early? What time?" Tamara asked. She was baffled because she told him she was picking him up today. She refused to show her surprise to the matter. "Oh, okay!"

She left the building, already dialing Jeff's number as she got in the car. He answered before the second ring, knowing she would be calling.

"What?" he snapped.

"You picked DJ up early?" she said as casually as she could. "I told you I was going to pick him up. What happened?"

"Yeah, I got him. I thought you would just stand him up like you have been for that bitch-ass nigga you're fucking with."

"Oh boy, here we go again. I thought we were so over that by now. When can I see my little brother, Jeff?"

"Never! You're never gonna see him again if it's up to me, bitch. I'm tired of this shit with you," he replied, getting straight to the point.

"Jeff, what are you talking about?"

"Bitch, you know exactly what the fuck I'm talking about. Don't play stupid. You wanna stay with that nigga instead of being home with DJ, then stay away for good.

Fuck it!"

"Jeff, where is DJ? I'm coming to get him."

"You dumb-ass bitch, what part don't you understand? You're not getting him."

"Don't make me call the cops on you, because I will," she threatened.

"And tell them what? That his father is taking care of him. Go ahead and do it," he said, daring her to do it.

"Please, I just want to see my lil brother. I miss him, Jeff," she pleaded.

"Fuck no! Now go ahead and live your life with your dirty-ass, broke-ass, drug-dealing boyfriend. I got him, and we're good. I hope you die with that nut-ass nigga!" he shouted with rage before ending the call.

Tamara stared at the phone in her hand, with no clue of what to do. She wanted so badly to see her brother, and she just had to figure out how.

~ ~ ~

It had been a long day for Tamara, and since Rico was busy with his partners, she decided to go back to work. Money was the only thing that could take her mind off what Jeff had said to her. She even thought about what he said for a brief moment. Was she wrong for messing with an older man? If he really loved her, why did he still have her working

in the massage parlor? All kinds of shit was going through her head.

As she was changing into her uniform, Tiffany came walking in the door counting money from her recent customers.

"Do you want to hang out tonight?" Tamara asked, trying to break the ice.

"I have something to do tonight. Maybe some other time," Tiffany replied, stuffing her money into her purse.

"Tamara, you have a customer in room 3. Are you ready?" the front desk hostess asked.

"Here I come now," she replied, checking her makeup. "Call me later if you're not busy."

"Whatever," Tiffany mumbled, watching Tamara heading to take care of her client.

Tamara walked into the room to find a man lying on her table facedown and naked, with only a towel covering him. She closed the door behind her and then walked over to the table. Once she removed her top, revealing her firm breasts, she grabbed the scented lotion.

"Would you like the VIP treatment?" she asked, leaning down, whispering in his ear. She started massaging his shoulders with her breasts resting on his arm.

"I just wanted to meet my daughter for the first time in over fourteen years," he replied, lifting his head up.

When Tamara saw his face, she jumped backward, trying

to cover herself. She hadn't seen her father since she was three. She immediately grabbed her shirt and threw it on.

"What are you doing here?"

"By the look on your face, I assume your mother never told you I was home, or never had the chance to," he smirked.

"I thought you were still in prison," she lied. The truth was she just hadn't wanted to see him.

"No, here I am in the flesh," he said, standing up, with the towel still over his midsection. "I know I haven't been in your life, but I want to change that now. Can we go somewhere and talk?"

"You have to leave because I'm working. I have nothing to say to you right now," Tamara said, walking out of the room and storming past Tiffany.

"That was quick," she said sarcastically.

Gene came out a few minutes later, fully dressed and looking for his daughter, but she was already gone. When he saw Tiff standing there in a thong, his dick suddenly had a mind of its own.

"What's your name, baby?" he asked, licking his lips.

"Not interested," she shot back, walking away. She made her ass clap because she knew he was staring. "Fucking two-minute man."

"Damn!" Gene said to himself. He shook his head and left the building. He had some other shit to take care of.

~ ~ ~

Tamara was locked in the bathroom bawling her eyes out. Everything was starting to become unbearable to her. She couldn't believe that her father just came into her workplace. It was at that moment she realized she was no longer gonna work there. Between her losing her mother, DJ's father taking him, and her own father trying to all of a sudden come back into her life, it was all starting to be too much for the seventeen-year-old. What she'd been through in the past year was more than what most young girls her age would ever experience in their lives.

She removed a small bag from her purse and held it in her hand. She just needed to take the pain away. Rico told her to share it with the workers, but to never take it herself. It seemed to calm all the other women down, and she wanted to feel the same way. She opened it up and then inserted it into the needle she was holding. She took the scrunchy out of her hair, wrapped her arm with it, and then inserted the needle into her veins. Once the substance from the needle entered her body, she felt a rush and was instantly in another world. She leaned back on the toilet and let the sensation of the drug come to her rescue.

TWENTY-THREE

Jeff was sitting in the living room in a discombobulated state. The pressure he had on his back right now made it hard for him to think properly. He knew he had started something that may be hard to get out of. Although he put himself in a situation, he was definitely not going to run somewhere and hide like a bitch. After that incident in the Fresh Grocer parking lot, he cut his two homies off. They had basically turned their backs on him when he needed them. He understood the nigga he had beef with was a very powerful man, but it was three against one. He looked even more like a sucker in front of his son.

Kayla came walking in the room, dragging his son by the hand. She quickly recognized the look on Jeff's face. Matter of fact, she had seen that face many times before on the faces of people scared for their lives. Seeing him like that could only mean he had gotten into some shit. She stopped right in front of him. He couldn't even face her right now. He got up and paced back and forth so he didn't have to face her.

"What's wrong, baby?" she asked with much concern.

"Shit crazy," he sighed. "I'm about to have some dangerous people on my ass, and it's gonna get real ugly. That's what's wrong."

"What people, and what have you done?" she asked,

giving him her full attention.

Kayla wasn't a dummy. She knew he had taken DJ from Tamara. Akira was her best friend, and when she started sleeping with Jeff, she kept it a secret from her. She felt bad about it, but at the same time her jealousy got the best of her. Akira had everything, and she wanted it.

"That bitch Tamara got that nigga Rico involved with family issues, so I told her she would never see her brother again."

"You can't keep that girl away from her lil brother, Jeff. That's wrong!"

"Whatever, fuck her and that nigga she running around with."

"Is that what it is? Are you jealous?"

"What you mean, am I jealous?" he snapped, getting defensive.

"Like I said, are you jealous because Rico is fucking her instead of you? I seen how you use to look at Tamara when I use to come see Akira," Kayla said, taunting him. "You wanted to fuck your own stepdaughter. Jeff, you are one sick motherfucker."

Before she could get another word out of her mouth, Jeff smacked the shit out of her. She stumbled backward, falling on the couch.

"Bitch I will kill you," he growled, gripping her by the neck and pulling her back up. He started choking the life out

of her.

"Get . . . the . . . fuck . . . off . . . of . . . me!" she screamed, trying to catch her breath. When she had an opening, she kicked him in the nuts.

"You bitch!" Jeff moaned, holding himself.

He punched Kayla dead in the mouth. She tried to block the next barrage of blows that followed, to no avail. He was like a man possessed as blow after blow rained from her face, down to her stomach. It was the sound of his son crying that snapped him out of his rage. If it wasn't for DJ, he would have killed Kayla.

"Bitch, don't you ever talk to me like that. If I ever see your face again, it will be the last time. If it wasn't for my son being here, I would have blown your fucking head off," he said, pulling his gun from his waist. He grabbed his son and left Kayla balled up in a fetal position, bleeding and hurting all over.

She reached for her phone sitting on the coffee table, then tried to make a call. Right before they answered, she passed out.

~ ~ ~

Ed decided to go out to the strip club to see his cousin. He hadn't seen her in two days, and she wasn't answering her phone. She had tried to call him, but he was in the shower

and didn't hear the call. He also was hoping that he would run into the nigga Rico. He wanted to confront the person that had stolen his girl, even though they weren't official yet.

As he stepped into the club, the smell of money was in the air. He was hoping to maybe run into one of his friends also. He thought it would be nice to see a familiar face. The last time he had seen Rico he was with Kayla, and it was about the work his man was robbed for. Ed did find out later that it was Kayla's fault. She was his peoples, so he was riding with her.

Ed made his way through the extremely packed club trying to find a spot to post up. He noticed that there were just as many girls in the club as men. He scanned the room looking for his cousin, but didn't see her. Just as he sat at a table, he saw a familiar face step in the club. It was Merv, and he had two bad women with him. It seemed like everybody in the club stopped moving except them. Merv's confident but sly demeanor screamed out for attention. Although the women with him didn't have on anything revealing, they were still just as beautiful and sexy as the other women. Everyone was staring at their asses.

"Hermes link, ice blue mink, tat on my wrist like I do not know what permanent is. They want me gone, wait for the kicker, bury me now I'll only get bigger, that's word to my niggas," Drake's new song "Gyalchester" burst through the speakers, causing all the strippers to turn up.

Ed continued watching Merv and the two beauties making their way through the crowd, until they stepped into the back office. When he looked again, he saw Rico emerge from the office, followed by three of his goons. Ed had to fight back the urge to react. Once the Drake song went off, the girls stopped dancing and moved on to the next customer. He looked around in awe at the massive amount of money that dudes had piled in front of them.

One of the dancers made their way over to him and started dancing seductively in a desperate attempt to get tipped. He quickly brushed her off, and then called her back to ask her a question.

"Have you seen Kayla, I mean Passion, lately?" he shouted over the loud music.

"No, not since the other day, baby," she replied, waiting for a tip.

Suddenly another dancer approached him. When he was able to see who it was, he smiled. It was Tiffany. The look on her face caused the other dancer to walk away. She stepped close to him, pressing her body against his.

"What the fuck you in here for? You trying to catch something?" she asked playfully.

Ed licked his lips before speaking. "I ain't trying to catch nothing here but you," he said, smacking her on the ass.

"In that case, let's get out of here then, when I get off the stage."

She made her way to the stage just as her music began to play. Once onstage, she turned on her seductive mode. She kept her eyes on Ed the whole time. She bent over, gripping her ankles. The tiny G-string was almost invisible the way it ran up the crack of her ass and disappeared. The further she bent over, the wider her ass spread.

Through her parted legs, she stared into Ed's eyes again. She wiggled her ass from side to side, making sure she had his full attention. Her ass had him hypnotized through all three songs. When she finished, she got dressed, then met him outside.

"Did you do that yet?" Ed asked once she was in the car.

"Yes, I did exactly what you asked me to do. I told her we were going to have some girl time. She's supposed to meet me tomorrow night."

"Perfect! I'ma teach that bitch to do me dirty," he replied pulling off.

"We going to the motel, my treat?" she asked, rubbing his dick. That was all she needed to do to get his attention. Once her head went into his lap, it was a wrap.

~ ~ ~

"I'm so glad you finally wanted to hang out," Tamara said. "I missed my best friend."

Tiffany could see a total change in her. It didn't take her

made a quick call and then got comfortable on the bed and waited.

Tamara stood at the sink and stuck her hand down her panties. She wiped across her pussy lips and then stuck her finger inside. She placed it up to her nose and sniffed, just to make sure she was on point. To no surprise, she wasn't anywhere near on point. She wet a rag and wiped herself free of the mild odor.

When she came out of the bathroom, Tiffany was standing there holding a cup for her. Tamara took a swig just to knock off the chill. She quickly removed her clothes and stood there naked.

"Do you have any more dope on you?" Tamara asked, pulling out money from her purse. She wanted to cop some from her for later so she wouldn't have to fuck the young dealer again like she did earlier.

"I have some coming. It will be here by the time we finish doing us."

"I don't get down like that, but you can only eat my pussy until the stuff comes, okay?"

"That's cool with me," Tiffany lied.

Tiff removed her clothes as Tamara lay on her back and spread her legs. Tiffany smiled at how pretty her pussy looked. Just the sight of it made her juices run down her leg. Tiffany slid up on the bed and kissed Tamara, running her tongue around her lips. Then she moved down Tamara's

body, her soft lips and tantalizing tongue sliding over her flesh, pausing at her breasts, where her tongue circled each nipple before her lips sucked it into throbbing erectness. Leaving a moist trail over her stomach, Tiffany parted Tamara's thighs, and Tamara groaned as she wound them around her neck. Tiff started kissing her pussy, licking, nibbling, and caressing it with her tongue. This was a whole other experience for Tamara, and she loved it.

"Damn, that feels so good," she moaned.

Tiffany's hands reached up to stroke her breasts as her mouth worked its sensuous magic on her pussy. Tamara's head rolled side to side, and her body twisted wildly. She felt her orgasm building up inside her, and then Tiffany stopped. She sat up and strapped on the dildo. At this point, the only thing on Tamara's mind was exploding. Tiff entered her, and Tamara gasped for air as she started pounding away.

Suddenly dots appeared before her eyes and a slight dizziness occurred. She thought she was having one hell of an orgasm. Tamara tried to shake the dizziness away, but it got worse. Then she thought that maybe she had drunk whatever was in that cup too fast. The sounds Tiff was making became faint. She looked around in shock wondering why she could barely hear. The room became a blur, and so did Tiffany. Her eyes got heavy, and she could barely keep them open. Her body felt light and relaxed, and she couldn't move a muscle. Suddenly the creaking of the

door caught her attention as two men entered.

"What took you so long?" Tiffany whispered.

The two men didn't say anything. Tamara felt as if she was hallucinating. Her brain was too frozen to even wrap her head around anything that was going on. By this time she was totally out of it, eyes barely open and ears deaf to any noise that was around her.

Her eyes closed shut for what seemed like seconds, but when they popped open she noticed the face of a stranger on top of her. She couldn't hear the noises that were coming from his mouth, but she could faintly see him smiling with pleasure as he bounced up and down on her. She could only focus on him for a matter of seconds before her eyes closed again.

When she opened her eyes again, this time she was lying on her stomach. She could feel the weight of something holding her down. She squirmed and wiggled, but the weight was too much for her. She looked over her shoulder and couldn't even make out the face of the other man who was behind her, driving himself in and out of her. Even though she was dazed and confused, she finally realized what was happening to her.

Her head flopped onto the pillow. She peeked up through one eye and saw her friend and the now familiar face standing over her, naked and laughing. Their mouths were stretched wide open as if they were yelling and cheering, but

she couldn't make out the words. In the midst of it all, she faded into a nod that quickly evolved into a deep slumber. She slept peacefully while the man behind her enjoyed her limp body.

~ ~ ~

Tamara woke up from her deep sleep quite groggy. She looked around the motel room and was baffled at how she had even gotten there. She looked down at her naked body and became even more confused. She sat at the edge of the bed, and her attention was caught by the used condoms lying on the bed leaking cum. She suddenly remembered Tiffany picking her up and them taking a ride.

Shortly after that the faces of the other two men popped into her mind. She could clearly remember them coming into the room. She also had the vision of them on top of and behind her sexually.

"Oh my God," she said knowing who it was that raped her. Tamara also realized Tiffany had slipped something into her drink causing her to pass out.

Tamara looked down just as a glob of semen plopped onto her foot. That skivvied her to no end. To see something like that freaked her out. Tears dripped down her eyes at a rapid pace, thinking how the people she trusted destroyed her life. It didn't help that she was becoming an addict at a young

age. She immediately dried her eyes, refusing to be the victim again. She was furious, and all she could think about was murder. Tamara grabbed her jeans and dug into her pockets for her money, but it was all gone.

"That little bitch," she yelled.

She felt like a total sucker as she got dressed. She called Rico and told him what happened and who did it. His anger could be felt through the phone as he snapped out. He let her know he was on his way, and ended the call. She promised herself that after this, she wasn't ever touching another drug again, or so she thought.

TWENTY-FOUR

Tiffany was walking out of the massage parlor after a long day of work. She had received several calls from Tamara, but didn't know what to say, so she didn't answer. She hopped in her car and pulled off, barely stopping at the stop sign. She sped down the block like a bat out of hell. She stared at the clock, shaking her head at the time. She bent a right at the corner without touching the gas pedal. The car swerved uncontrollably, but she caught the wheel with ease.

Tiffany quickly approached the intersection with no intention of even stopping at the red light. She looked to the right, and just as she did, a vehicle came at her from her blind side on the left. The vehicle missed the nose of her car by less than a few inches. Tiffany looked to her left with her heart pounding. The car had her path blocked. A masked gunman popped out from the passenger's seat of the car, causing her rapidly pounding heart to stop beating. She froze in fear as the gunman approached the car.

"Move, bitch, and I will blow your fucking brains out," he said aiming the gun at her window.

Tiff put her hands high in the air, in submission. She thought they were some stickup kids trying to rob her.

"Here, take the car!" she shouted when he snatched the door open.

He dragged her from the car and flung her toward the second gunman, who had appeared throughout the turmoil. One man hopped into the driver's seat of her car, while the other dragged Tiffany to the car in front of them.

"No, no! Please!" Tiff cried as she was thrown into the backseat. The driver of the car peeled off with a quickness, and Tiffany's car tailed right behind it.

~ ~ ~

Tiffany sat on the floor blindfolded by a black T-shirt. Her mouth was gagged with a pair of her own panties. She had no clue what this was about.

"Where's her phone?" Rico whispered when he walked through the door.

"I'm already on it, boss. I tossed that shit on the way here. They won't be tracking that shit," he replied.

"Good thinking," Rico whispered. "I see I taught y'all well."

One of his men paced in circles around Tiffany, who was sitting in the chair, rocking back and forth. Rico took one long look at her with not a bit of compassion. Finally, he walked over to her and smacked the shit out of her. He then took the blindfold off and stared at her. As soon as she saw who was standing in front of her, she damn near peed on herself. There was no doubt in her mind that she had fucked

up.

"Bitch, you want to live, right?" he asked. Tiffany nodded her head up and down as tears flowed from her eyes, soaking the T-shirt. "I thought so, but don't cry now. You wasn't crying when you set my girl up to get assaulted. Call that nigga Ed, and if you do as you're told, you may just leave out of here unscathed."

He placed the phone in her hand. She held it tightly like it was a lifesaver. Rico's man aimed his gun at her, waiting for her to comply.

"Dial, bitch," he said as he put the gun up to her forehead. Tiffany could barely dial the numbers on the tiny prepaid phone. She began dialing clumsily. She held it in the air, waiting for the next instructions. "Tell him you have a nigga here with a lot of money on him, and that he needs to hurry up if he wants it."

She did exactly as she was told, putting Ed on speakerphone. Just like the greedy, money-hungry person he was, Ed fell for the bait. He told her to keep the guy occupied until he arrived. She agreed and then told him the address before ending the call.

"Now you better hope he comes," Rico told her. "Your life depends on it."

"I'm sorry for what happened to Tamara. I didn't know he was going to do that. I swear," she said.

"It's a little too late for apologies. I'm not the one who

needs it, anyway."

Rico slid the back of the prepaid phone open and removed the battery so it couldn't be tracked back to them. Anxiety was ripping through his entire body. It only happened when it was time to kill. He walked around to alleviate the butterflies in his gut. The first few phases of his plan had been executed successfully. Now it was time to prepare for his next guest, who should be arriving soon.

~ ~ ~

An hour later Ed's car pulled up in front of the building. Rico's goon squad was waiting inside a bombed-out Chevy Lumina. As soon as he stepped out of the car, they swooped him, punching and kicking him in the face and head. After the beat down, they dragged him inside to join Tiffany, who was in the corner of the room, blindfolded, sitting in a pool of blood. The smell of fresh blood was stomach turning. What looked like enough blood to be from a murder victim was the blood from Tiffany's monthly menses.

The excruciating cramps that she was experiencing, was nothing compared to the fear she felt. The creaking of the door set her on alert. When the goons finished tying Ed up next to Tiffany, Rico and Tamara walked in. The sight of the blood made them think the goons had already killed one of them without their permission. Rico looked at his crew with

disappointment on his face.

"What the fuck?" Rico mumbled. Tamara didn't look phased one bit about the blood on the floor.

"The bitch is on her period. She's been bleeding like a pig since earlier."

"Good," Tamara said, taking charge of the scene. She removed the blindfold and the gag from Tiffany's mouth and then smacked the dog shit out of her. "You gone let this dirty-dick nigga rape me after all that shit I've been through."

"Please, Tamara, I didn't know that was gonna happen. I thought you said you would let me go if I called and got him over here."

"We lied!" Rico laughed at how naive she was. "Bitch, you ain't going anywhere but to hell."

Tamara grabbed the scissors from her purse and then cut off Ed's clothes, leaving him sitting there butt naked. She took his boxers and wiped up Tiffany's blood and then stuffed the bloody boxers in his mouth. She then placed some duct tape over his mouth so he couldn't scream. The goons watched her in disgust as she then heated up a knife on the hotplate.

"Since you like raping people, I'm gonna make it so you can't rape anyone else," she said with anger in her voice. "And you, since those dick suckers can't tell the truth, I have something for you too."

She walked over to Ed and then kneeled down in front of him. She started sucking on his dick until he was nice and hard. Then, in one swift motion, she took the red-hot knife and sliced his dick off. Ed screamed out in pain, but the muffled sound fell on deaf ears. All the men standing around, including Rico, gagged. She wasn't done yet though. She took his severed penis and stuffed it in Tiffany's mouth, and then she took the knife and slit her throat.

"Oh shit!" Rico said at the atrocious sight. "Remind me not to ever piss you off," he joked.

"Let's get out of here," she said, heading for the door.

"Clean this mess up, and have the cleaners take care of the bodies."

"What about him? He's still breathing," one of his men asked.

Boom! Boom! Boom!

"Not for long," Rico replied, holding the smoking gun in his hand. He tucked it back in his waist, and then him and Tamara left the goons to do their jobs.

TWENTY-FIVE

Instead of the cleaners getting rid of both bodies, they left Ed's body in the middle of the hood to make a statement, and everybody understood it. Rico wasn't done yet though. He wanted people to know not to mess with anyone on his team. It was make-a-statement time.

Jeff sat on the edge of the bed, staring at the television, which was muted, while he sipped on his morning coffee. Kayla lay nestled up in the covers, after hours of hot sex. Since Akira was gone, she had been getting real close with Jeff. A familiar house flashed across the television screen and captured Jeff's attention. His mouth dropped as he recognized the place. It was the area where he met up with Ed. When his picture popped up on the screen, he quickly increased the volume to listen to the details. The words that came out of the reporter's mouth seemed unreal.

"Edward Jones of Southwest Philly was found dead in the middle of the street, in the Bartram Village projects, for everyone to see. It was a very gruesome scene, as his genitals were severed from his body. The medical examiners are still looking for the missing parts. Police have no witnesses at this time and are asking for your help. Please call the police headquarters or the hotline at the bottom of the screen if you have any information that would lead to the arrest and conviction of the person or people behind this heinous

crime," the reporter said.

Kayla lifted up, wide awake at the mention of her cousin's name. She watched on as the reporter showed more pictures of the crime scene. The tears started flowing freely from her eyes as she tried to process the news.

"Oh my God, not my little cousin," she sobbed.

It all became a blur for Kayla after that. Jeff tried comforting her, but it was no use. DJ came into their room, and when he saw Kayla crying, he ran over to her. He held her tightly as if he was trying to take her pain away.

"It's gonna be okay," Jeff said. He wasn't really the emotional type, but he was feeling just a bit of sympathy for her.

Jeff left the room, and once he stepped into the hallway, his demeanor changed. He leaned his head back, looking at the ceiling, and inhaled deeply. Deep breaths were not even enough to ease the tension he was feeling. He wondered what had happened to Ed and why. His mind was racing a mile a minute, and he wondered if Tiffany had heard about it yet. He took out his phone and made the call to Tiff.

~ ~ ~

The small church was packed with so many people, they barely had room to walk. All his friends were there to see him off. There were a lot of the neighborhood drug dealers in attendance, but only because they were trying to see if

someone really cut his dick off. The hood thought it was one of his crazy girlfriends. Only a few people there shed tears; the others were desensitized to death because murders took place every day. Instead of sobbing and mourning, most of them used the gathering as a place of networking and a mere social event. The few family members that were there tried to block out the commotion and mourn the deceased.

Ed's body lay in the coffin dressed in a black suit. He was going to be laid to rest honorably, despite how dishonorably he had died. A few of the women he fucked were sprinkled around the room displaying sorrow. His male friends who loved him were full of sorrow as well, but refused to show it.

In the midst of all the socializing and the little mourning, a masked Rico peeked through the doorway and made a quick assessment of the room. Merv, dressed in all black, with a black skully covering his face, stepped up next to him. Rico was armed with a handgun, while Merv gripped an AR-15 in one hand. Herb and one of his men waited outside in the car for them so they could make a quick getaway.

"You ready to handle this?" Merv asked.

"Let's do it," Rico replied.

Merv darted into the room, aiming his assault rifle randomly, just to keep the people in the room at bay. Loud screaming pierced the air. Merv squeezed rounds into the air, shooting out light fixtures and lacing the ceiling with holes. The AR sounded off rapidly. People were screaming their

heads off as they dove onto the floor for cover.

The sound of three consecutive gunshots from a handgun interrupted the rapid sounds of the assault weapon.

Boc! Boc! Boc!

Rico stood directly over the coffin, firing shots into it. He continued firing into the casket, bullets being dumped into the already dead body. To further disrespect the dead, Rico kicked the coffin as hard as he could, knocking it over. More screaming could be heard as the coffin rolled off the wheels and fell to the floor, landing on its side.

Ed's body rolled out of the casket, and he landed on his face. The screaming got louder as the place was in a uproar. Merv dumped two more shots into the back of Ed's head. He kicked the dead corpse a couple of times before taking off toward the door. Rico, still standing at the door, continued to aim at the people, giving Merv time to exit the room.

He finally exited the room, leaving everyone in total shock of what had just happened. A few brave men ran to the front of the room, but it was already too late. Both men had fled the funeral parlor and were out of sight. The people in the room had never witnessed anything as disrespectful as this, and wondered who and why someone would do something so coldhearted.

"That should teach these motherfuckers a lesson," Rico chuckled. Even though Ed was already dead, he hoped they had killed his spirit as well.

TWENTY-SIX

It had been almost three months since the death of Ed and the mysterious disappearance of Tiffany. People thought she left town because she owed some dangerous people money, but only Rico and a select few knew the truth of her whereabouts. Rico's team had fed her to the sharks and all the other creatures of the sea.

After doing all that for Tamara, he found out that she was still using dope. That was something he didn't tolerate, and when he gave her the ultimatum to get clean, she took it. However, it was short-lived. He caught her in the bathroom at the club giving some dude head while they both shot up. This time he treated her like the whore she had become, and put her to work. She was getting ready to hit the stage when Rico came walking into the dressing room.

"Why are you still sitting here? Get your ass out on that floor."

"I'm going. I just need a little pick-me-up to get me through the night," she said, walking over to where he was standing. She got down on her knees in front of him and placed her mouth on the crotch of his pants. "Let me take care of you real quick, daddy."

"You wanna take care of me?"

"Yes," she said, unzipping his jeans with her teeth.

She somehow managed to remove his dick with her

tongue and place it inside her mouth. The warmness of her saliva had him giving in to her once again. Without using her hands, she gave him the best blowjob he ever had. Rico shot his load down her throat in a matter of minutes.

"Now get yourself together and get the fuck out on the floor and make my money," he said, fixing his clothes back and walking out of the dressing room.

When Rico walked into his office, Kayla was sitting on the couch. He wondered where the hell she had been hiding.

"What the fuck do you want? You think you can just come and go when you feel like it?" he stated, sitting down at his desk.

"It's a long story, but I would like my job back, please."

"Go get ready, but this is the last time I do this. The next time you're gone this long, stay gone, and I mean that shit," he spat.

Kayla walked out and headed for the dressing room. Rico opened up the safe and proceeded to count the take from the previous night. He was gonna drop it in the bank when he left. A couple minutes later, there was another knock on the door.

"Damn it," he said, heading toward the door. "Didn't I say not to bother me when I'm counting my—" As soon as he opened the door, he was met with a barrage of bullets.

Boca! Boca! Boca! Boca!

The music from the club was so loud that it muffled the sound from the weapon. Rico fell backward, hitting his head

on the edge of the desk. The shooter stepped in, closed the door, and then stood over the top of Rico. His eyes were wide open as if he was trying to speak, but nothing came out but globs of blood. The shooter aimed at his chest and fired two more shots at close range. Rico's eyes rolled into the back of his head.

"That's for my cousin," Kayla said, standing there with the smoking gun.

She pulled out a bag from her purse and rushed over to the safe. She loaded up as much of the money as would fit in there. Once she was done, she headed out to the back door, where her accomplice was waiting.

"Everything good?"

"Yeah, that went easier than I thought. There's enough money in that bag for us to leave and start all over again, baby."

"What about his partners? You know they will come for us. The three of us needs to get out of here now."

"I have one last thing to take care of. Give me ten minutes and I'll be back," she stated, heading back inside.

"Coming to the stage is one of the sexiest dancers we have to offer. Believe me, you're not gonna want to miss this," the DJ stated, hyping the crowd up for what was to come. "All you men and ladies, get those bills ready for the sexy Mocha."

"Freak show, freak show, bounce that ass, make your knees touch your elbows. Freak show, freak show . . ."

Once Future came through the speakers, everyone gathered around the stage with their bills in hand, trying to see the performance. Tamara hit the stage, climbing up the pole and then sliding down it without using her hands. When she touched the bottom, she did a split, giving the audience a firsthand sight of her swollen pussy lips. The crowd cheered her on when she started twerking her ass upside down. Money was being tossed onstage like paper.

Kayla heard all the cheering and wanted to see who was causing such a commotion. Since this was her first day back, she didn't get a chance to see all the new girls yet because they were on the floor attending to customers. She walked up to one of the girls she did know, and stood beside her.

"She's killing that shit for a newbie. She had to do this before, or she had a lot of practice," Ice said with a smile.

Kayla smiled at her friend's statement and was about to walk away to make the call she needed to make, until she saw who the new girl was. Her smile quickly turned into shock. It was Tamara!

"I always knew she would follow in her mother's footsteps," she said to herself.

"What?" Ice replied, confused.

"Nothing!" Kayla told her, walking away.

This was too good to be true. She was about to kill two birds with one stone. It didn't get any better than that, she thought. Kayla waited for Tamara to finish her set, and when she was done, she followed her back to the dressing room.

"Hey, Tamara, Rico said come to his office now."

"Okay!" Tamara said cheerfully. "Oh, and sorry about your cousin." Kayla just nodded, but didn't even respond.

Tamara thought Rico wanted to finally give her another chance, and rushed up to see him with a smile on her face. When she opened the door, horror hit her dead in the face. Rico was slumped over on the floor, dead from gunshots wounds.

She turned around to scream, but was staring down the barrel of a gun. Kayla had a sinister look in her eyes.

"What, you thought I didn't know it was you and Rico that killed my cousin?" she asked.

"He raped me, Kayla. Him and Tiffany drugged me and then raped me, so they got what they deserved."

"Wait a minute! What do you mean *they* got what they deserved?" she questioned. "What happened to Tiffany?"

At that moment, Tamara knew she had just fucked up. Nobody knew anything about Tiffany's whereabouts. She had just admitted that she did something to Tiffany also.

"I don't know what you're talking about," she replied, trying to save face.

"So you killed Tiffany too?" Kayla said, pointing the gun at her. "Let's go, bitch. I'm gonna let you watch me kill your lil brother before I kill you."

Kayla's plan at first was to set them up in a murder/suicide, but when she found out that Tamara also killed Tiffany, the plan changed. Now this was very

personal. She didn't have to worry about any repercussions, because they were going to kill her lil brother anyway.

"Please don't do this."

"Shut up and move," Kayla said, pushing her toward the back door.

When they stepped outside, Kayla forced her to the car that was waiting for them. As they got close, something caught Kayla's eye that didn't look right. As soon as they approached the car, Tamara could see the man's head cocked to the side. She didn't think anything of it until they were standing directly in front of it.

"Oh my God!" Tamara screamed at the sight of Jeff's dead body. He had a bullet hole to the head.

"What's the—?" Kayla was about to say, until she saw Jeff. She turned toward Tamara, aiming the gun at her. "You did this, bitch. I'm a kill you."

"Freeze! Police! Drop the gun now."

Kayla looked around at all the cops with their weapons aimed at her. She didn't know what to do, so she pulled Tamara close to her, with her gun pointed at her head.

"Get away from me or she dies," Kayla yelled.

The officers started backing up, trying not to spook her into pulling the trigger. She looked around, but had no place to run. She held onto Tamara tightly out of fear of one of those trigger-happy pigs killing her.

"Ma'am, you have nowhere to go. Drop your weapon!" the sergeant hollered out.

"Please don't kill me," Tamara pleaded.

Even though she had committed murder, she was still scared to death of leaving her brother here by himself. She had no choice but to cooperate with Kayla. She knew the cops weren't going to let her get away. Just as things couldn't get any worse, they did. All of a sudden there were four muffled sounds, and four officers fell to the ground. Another series of muffled sounds followed, and down went the remaining three cops. Kayla smiled, already knowing what had happened, and hit the trunk button on the car.

"Get in now," she said, pushing Tamara away from her. After what she had just witnessed, there was no doubt in her mind that if she didn't do as she was told, she would be next. "Move it!"

Kayla watched her climb inside the trunk, and slammed it shut. She had to get out of there, and fast. She dragged Jeff's body out of the driver's seat, jumped in, and then sped off before more cops arrived.

~ ~ ~

Herb and Merv couldn't believe what happened in their club. They would definitely be shut down for a long time. It was a good thing the building wasn't in their name, or all the heat would come down on them. Neither one could have that with all the drug activity they were into.

"We're gonna have to shut that club down eventually.

There's no way we will ever be able to operate with all that drama that bitch caused," Herb stated as they watched the video.

"I want the bitch that caused this dead, and get rid of that tape. If they ask about our cameras, they don't work," Merv said.

His crew all nodded in agreement and then headed out of the office. Merv sat down at the table where they had topless women wearing only panties bagging up dope. Herb poured a drink and then walked over as well.

"I never knew women could cause so much trouble. What happened to the days where all you had to worry about was them cheating?" Herb asked.

"Shit, those days are over, bro," Merv replied. "These bitches want to act like niggas, so we have to treat them accordingly. It's time we stepped back on the streets and showed motherfuckers that we still get our hands dirty."

"Who the fuck was she with though? They took out seven fucking cops without any problem. I think we need them on the team," Herb joked. "Seriously, we can't have this kind of heat around our spot. It's bad for business."

"Our people is handling it," Merv assured him.

"Alright, I'm out, bro. I'll see you tomorrow, 'cause I have a date."

"Be safe!"

"I will," Herb assured him, patting his shoulder holster, letting him know he was strapped. They shook hands, and

then Herb rolled out.

Merv sat there watching the girls work. One particular girl had his attention though. She had an ass like a stallion. Even though she was sitting down in the chair, he could still see it by the way she leaned forward.

"Excuse me, shorty, what's your name?"

"Yo no hablo ingles (I do not speak English)," she responded.

"Cuál es su nombre? (What is your name?)"

"Mi nombe es Maria (My name is Maria)," she said.

As long as the girls had been working for them, they never heard him speak Spanish. Now here he was speaking it so fluently. A couple of them even wondered if he had been listening to their conversations. Merv knew what they were thinking, and smiled. He came over to talk to her.

"Tu es bien wapa. ¿Tienes un hombre en tu vida? (You are very beautiful. Do you have a man in your life?)" Merv whispered in her ear, causing her to chuckle.

"No soy solo. ¿Por qué? (No, I am single. Why?)" she replied shyly.

"Porque quiero llevaste para atras y romperte culo (Because I want to take you back and break your ass)," Merv said stated boldly.

"¿Tu esea ta atrenido con t odo las mujeresque conoce? (Do you have sex with all the women you know?)" Maria blushed. Her pussy was getting moist just listening to the way he was talking to her.

"Unico las que yo quiero mucho (Only the ones I love very much)."

"Si es asi, coja lo que tu quiera (If it is so, take what you want)," she whispered back in a seductive tone that gave Merv an instant erection.

"Eso lo que quiero ohir (That's what I want to do)," he replied, rubbing her back, sending chills down her spine.

Merv stood up and started walking away. He turned around and motioned for Maria to come with him. She stared at him as if to say, "Now?" He waved her over again.

"Y esto (And that)?" she asked, pointing to the dope she had been bagging up.

"Desa que ello tesmine aciendo ego. ¿Tu vas a vemir? (Let this testify to the ego. Are you coming?)"

"Espero que llegue pronto (I hope I will be soon)," she said, licking her lips.

That was all Merv needed to hear. Maria threw on her shirt and skirt and then followed him outside to his SUV that was parked in front of the door. He needed to be alone with this beauty. Since his vehicle's tint was limo dark, he wasn't worry about being seen. They climbed in the backseat and shut the door.

He removed her shirt, exposing her C-cup breasts once again. Merv started kissing and licking on her nipples while playing with them. Maria was mesmerized as he took off his pants and underwear. He placed her hand on his erection. It was already rock hard and pulsating. He slid her forward in

the seat a little and then straddled her chest, sticking his dick in her face.

Maria licked the tip at first and then took his whole dick into her mouth. She sucked his dick and licked his balls for a few minutes, and then he placed her over the seat on her stomach. He lifted the back of her skirt over her ass and pulled her panties down her legs around her knees. She could feel his hot dick rubbing against her ass.

"Oh, popi, mmmm, *si*," she moaned, reaching between her legs to guide his erection inside of her warm pussy. Maria screamed out, mumbling something in Spanish as he fucked her slowly and sensually, and then sped up.

Her pussy was so wet that his dick was sliding in and out with ease. Maria reached down and played with his balls and then rubbed the spot between his dick and asshole. After several minutes of his dick stretching her pussy apart, he pulled out. He buried his face in her dripping hole from behind. She held his head while grinding her pussy against his face and tongue. She told him how good his tongue was, but she needed his dick back inside her. He urgently obliged!

Merv was knocking her back out, making the SUV rock like a cradle. She could feel his abdomen slamming hard into her ass cheeks. He sped up even faster when he felt himself about to explode inside her walls. When he shot his load, so did Maria. Merv pulled out of her, his cum running down her legs, and fixed his pants. He sat there, trying to get himself together.

"Damn, your shit was good. We have to do this again."

"Yo no hablo ingles (I do not speak English)," she said, shaking her head.

"Oh shit, I forgot you can't speak English, ma," Merv replied. "Diablo, que son buenos. Debemos hacer esto otra vez. ¿Quieres seguir trabajando conmigo? (Devil, you are good. We have to do this again. Do you want to keep working for me?)"

Maria moved close to him, pulling his dick back out of his pants. She started massaging it with her hand, bringing him back to a semi erection.

"¿Quieres otro sabor? (You want another taste?)" she said, her emerald eyes staring into his.

"Eso me vustaria (That I would like)," Merv said, scooting down as Maria wrapped her juicy lips around his now fully resurrected penis. All he could do was close his eyes and enjoy what this Spanish fly was doing to him.

TWENTY-SEVEN

"Hey, you! Wake up," Kayla yelled, throwing water in Tamara's face. Tamara opened her eyes and looked around the room. All she could see was another chair, and a bed. It was who was lying on that bed that got her attention. It was her little brother, sleeping peacefully. She tried to get loose from the restraints, to no avail. "Don't worry, he will be just fine if you do exactly what you're supposed to."

"DJ!" Tamara screamed out. He didn't even move, let alone answer. The effects of whatever Kayla had done to her were starting to wear off. But all she could remember was seeing Jeff's dead body and then the cops that tried to help her being gunned down before she got inside the trunk of a car. "What did you do to my brother?"

"I gave him something to help him sleep peacefully. That's not important right now. What is important is what I need you for. Someone paid me a lot of money to grab you for them. Do you know what money does to me?" Kayla paused, squeezing her legs together. She closed her eyes momentarily, then opened them back up. "Anyway, you will find out in a few minutes who went through all this trouble just for you."

"Please, just let us go," Tamara pleaded.

"You won't be going anywhere when this is all over,"

Kayla said, pulling up a chair and sitting right across from her. "See, the thing is, you killed my cousin, and you admitted to killing Tiffany, you little slut. You really think I'm gonna let that slide?"

"Kayla, you don't have to do this. I just want to take my little brother home, please. I told you that they drugged and raped me. What was I supposed to do, huh?"

"Don't give me that sob story. I'm not trying to hear that shit right now. While we're waiting, since you want to be a whore, you might as well get fucked like one."

Kayla pulled out a needle that was filled with dope. Tamara was trying to stay clean, but the sight of the needle made her mouth water.

"What are you gonna do with that?"

"This is to calm you down, for my little surprise," Kayla said. She grabbed Tamara's foot and stuck the needle between her toes, shooting her up with the dope.

It didn't take long for the substance to take effect on her. It was like a rush, making her whole body tingle. Her pussy instantly became moist, causing her to have an orgasm.

"I have a secret for you, little Ms. Prissy. I'm the one who killed your mother," Kayla whispered in Tamara's ear.

It didn't process in her brain yet, because the drug had taken her over, causing her to have poor judgment. Kayla untied her and made her get on her hands and knees. She then walked out of the room and came back in with a German

shepherd on a leash. Kayla positioned the dog behind Tamara, and as if on cue, the dog climbed up behind Tamara like he already knew what to do. He started humping on her as his pink penis grew, ready to enter Tamara.

"What the fuck are you doing?" a voice yelled from behind, causing Kayla to jump.

"Just having fun."

"Are you fucking crazy? How would you like it if I made him fuck your psychotic ass?" he said, walking toward her. Tamara still only had on her stripping outfit, so when he saw her, it took everything in him not to snap out. "Get her some clothes to put on now."

When Tamara looked up with hazy eyes and saw who was standing there, she started crawling over toward him.

"So is this what you wanted all this time but couldn't get?" Tamara asked, sitting up and rubbing her pussy. She put a finger inside, then stuck it in her mouth, tasting her own juices.

"Get your ass up," he snapped. When Kayla came back with some clothes, he grabbed her by the neck. "What the fuck did you give her?"

"Just something to calm her down. It will wear off in an hour or two. I'm sorry," she replied, scared to death. She could barely breathe with his hand around her neck. When he finally let go, she started gasping for air.

"After we handle this business, I'm gone," he said,

helping Tamara get dressed. She was now out of it, so he laid her next to her brother. "Keep an eye on them and don't do anything stupid. Can you manage to do that? After all, I did kill that nigga Jeff so he'd never find out whose that really was." He left out to put the final part of the plan together.

~ ~ ~

Merv was so into Maria that he decided to take her out for dinner. They ended up going to his favorite restaurant out in Delaware. When they walked into the Cheesecake Factory, Ada showed them to their seat. Merv asked for the waitress that always waited on him, and when she came over, she smiled.

"How are you?" she asked.

"I'm good, Jalissa. My friend doesn't speak English, so you have to talk to her in Spanish," he said, opening up the menu. Maria did the same, but didn't know what it said.

"¿Que quiere comer? (What do you want to eat?)" Jalissa asked.

Maria ordered the smoked salmon with teriyaki sauce and the lemon rice pilaf. Merv ended up getting a well-done steak with mashed potatoes. Jalissa came back to see what they wanted to drink.

"Yo quiero una botella de Cîroc y la mujer un Martini de manzana (I want a bottle of Cîroc, and an apple martini for

the woman)," he told her, and she walked away to retrieve their drinks.

As they sat there conversing, Merv received a phone call. He pulled out his iPhone from his pocket.

"Yo," Merv said, not recognizing the number.

"What's up, nigga?" a man whispered.

"Who this?" Merv asked with uncertainty.

"Don't worry about all that. All you need to know is that we got your niece."

"What the fuck are you talking about?" Merv asked, getting up from his seat and stepping outside so no one could hear his conversation.

"What I'm talking about is Tamara. Don't worry, she's safe as long as we get what we want. I know your mind is going crazy right now, but if you want to see her again, act right."

"Yo, who is this? If this is some kind of joke, someone will pay with their lives," Merv snapped.

"This ain't no fucking prank. Fuck you think I am? This is some real shit. Now unless you want me to send you a body part for proof, I suggest you listen."

"You must not know who the fuck I am. I have shooters all over this city, and everywhere else, for that matter. When I find you, you and your family is dead," Merv shouted with venom in his voice.

Merv was trying to figure out how someone knew he had

a niece. There were only two people that knew about that, and that was his brother, who was incarcerated right now, and his partner. It wasn't adding up. He tried catching the voice, but it was muffled.

"Yeah, yeah, yeah, I know what you're capable of, and you should know what I'm capable of," he interrupted.

"Herb?" Merv said, finally catching on to something he said. "Nigga, I know this better be a fucking game."

"Now that you know who this is, you know how serious I am. I want you to turn over all of your investments, sign over your half of all the real estate in Delaware and Atlanta to me."

"Are you out of your fucking mind?"

"No, I'm very sane, thank you. You really thought I didn't know you had side deals going on without me? I know everything, and if you value her life, you'll call Gene and tell him to bring that paperwork."

"Gene is in prison," Merv said, confused.

"Damn, you really don't know shit about your fam, do you? He's been out for a minute now. Why don't y'all get y'all affairs in order, and when I call back be ready to do business."

"Nig—" Merv managed to say before Herb ended the call.

He looked at his phone, trying to figure out what made his long-time friend and partner turn on him like this. What

bugged him even more was the fact that Herb knew his brother was home. That was something Merv didn't even know. Then they had his niece that no one knew about, held captive somewhere.

"Popi," Maria said, coming up behind him.

"Uno momento," he said, rushing back inside to pay for their food.

When he came back out, they rushed to his vehicle and headed back to Philly. He called his team and told them to meet him at the spot. It was wartime, but this time it would be different. He would be going up against someone that knew him just as well as he knew them.

TWENTY-EIGHT

Merv paced the room in a distraught manner. In the room with him were two of his most trusted killers. Loyalty was deeply instilled in them. Merv could rely on them to never turn against him, and they knew he would die for them. Neither of them were prepared for this because they never even fathomed the thought. They'd participated in plenty of kidnap situations, but never had it been close enough to them to even give it much thought. Karma was bitch, and she had just come back with vengeance.

"This motherfucker has just crossed the line, so it's time to clap back. He must have forgotten who he was dealing with. If he harms my niece, I will destroy everything or anyone that he calls family or home," Merv said with rage. "Why hasn't my fucking brother gotten here yet?"

Both men watched their boss, with a million thoughts running through their minds. Whoopie was the first to speak.

"Big homie, we can't take that threat lightly. Bottom line is, he has her, but we don't know where they are. They could be held up anywhere."

Just as he finished his statement, Gene came running through the door. He looked at his brother for a minute before saying anything.

"I apologize for not coming sooner. I thought I would be able to come here, see my daughter, and get back before my

PO noticed that I left the city. Now none of that even matters to me. I want my daughter back," he stated, punching the wall.

"Calm down, bro. We're going to handle this shit accordingly," Merv replied. "I'm calling one of my contacts now, to find out what they know. We will find her."

Merve wanted to curse Gene out for being home all this time without letting him know, but now wasn't the time. After he made a few calls, Merv sent his crew a picture of Tamara. Merv set his phone down on the table, then poured a drink. One of the girls bagging up pointed to the picture, causing Gene to look.

"I think she's seen her before," Gene said. "Everybody get out except her."

"They only speak Spanish," Whoopie replied.

"Merv, get them out of here, bro," Gene demanded.

Merv looked at the women and relayed the message: "Deja el trabajo sobre la mesa y sal de la mierda (Leave the work on the table and get the hell out).

The women immediately jumped up from the table.

"Tú, ven a hablar conmigo por un minute (You, come speak with us for a minute)."

The girl that had seen the picture stayed behind. Gene showed her the picture again trying to find out what she knew.

"Ask her where did she see this woman?"

"¿Adonde viste esta mujer? (Where did you see this

woman?)"

"Ella estaba con un tipo an la calle mountain," she replied nervously.

"She said she was on Mountain Street with some dude," Merv replied. He asked her a couple more questions and she answered them. Afterward, Gene slid her three hundred-dollar bills, and then all of them strapped up with high-power weapons.

"I told that nigga I wasn't signing shit over to him, and now we're gonna show him why. Load up and let's end this shit," Merv said, cocking the MAC-11.

The four of them hopped into the stolen Dodge Magnum Gene picked up on his way there, and headed to South Philly with murder on their minds.

~ ~ ~

Kayla got out the shower and oiled herself all over before slipping into a raspberry-colored lace cami. Since she hadn't fucked Herb in a while, she decided to give him a taste of what he'd been missing. Since Tamara and DJ were in the basement, she knew they wouldn't be disturbed. She crept upstairs toward Herb's room. She was on a dick mission and could snort it out like a dope fiend could dope.

The door to his room was ajar just enough for her to slip through without making a noise. Kayla closed it as quietly as she could behind her. She moved toward the bed,

excitement rising from her lips all the way down to her pussy. She slid her thong off and then crawled over to him.

"Kayla, what are you doing?" Herb asked, waking up just as she was straddling him.

"I came to take care of you and show my appreciation for letting me be a part of this take over," she replied.

She lowered her pussy to the curve of his mouth. He knew the routine, so there was no need for her to walk him through what was about to go down. She opened up her feverish pussy and practically fed it to him.

"Ummm," Herb moaned, surrendering without a fight. He knew this was wrong to do right now because of everything that was going on. Then he thought about his goon squad that was guarding the perimeter, and let his little head think for him.

"I've missed this! Damn, that feels so fucking good," Kayla whispered, loving the way his tongue stretched the folds of her yoni.

In between licks, Herb stuck a finger in her asshole, intensifying the pleasure. She reached behind and stroked his dick as he continued eating her out. He feasted on her pussy a while longer before she decided she wanted to reciprocate the favor. She turned around so their bodies molded into a sixty-nine position. Kayla started gunning him down, forcing him into one of the craziest orgasms he ever had. As he shot his load down her throat, she released her own juices.

"Shit, you still got it!"

"No doubt," Herb replied, rubbing her breasts.

"Does that mean I can get some dick, too?"

Without saying a word, he took complete charge, spreading her legs and positioning himself over her. He eased into her love tunnel and went to work, giving her orgasm after orgasm until they both fell asleep.

~ ~ ~

After receiving the information where the Spanish chick had seen Tamara, Merv, Gene, and Merv's crew cruised down the block hoping to run into somebody. They all were locked and loaded, weapons in hand, safeties off. They spotted a couple of Herb's goons standing around smoking cigarettes.

"Let me out. I'm gonna smoke every nigga on his team until I find my daughter," Gene stated, snatching his gun from his lap and reaching for the door handle.

"Calm down, bro," Merv said as he gripped his gun. "If they're holding her in that house, we'll get her. Just follow my lead."

They drove past them, trying not to alarm them. Once they reached the corner, Merv and Gene hopped out. They gave Merv's two goons a chance to drive around the block so they could box them in. As Merv and Gene eased up the block, his men approached from the other end. They pulled up in front of Herb's two men and then jumped out. The two

men's eyes popped out of their heads as they stood face-to-face with death. Merv and Gene ran up on them with their guns drawn.

"Where is my daughter?" Gene asked. He reached out to grab one of the men, but was surprised when the man spun around, gun in hand. The man fired trying to save his own life.

Bocka! Blocka!

That's the only two shots Herb's goons were able to get off, before Merv and his men shredded their bodies to pieces with bullet after bullet. They were dead before they even hit the ground.

"Let's go!" Merv yelled, running toward the building they were in front of.

~ ~ ~

"What was that?" Herb said, jumping up. Kayla quickly followed, grabbing her clothes. They both rushed out of the bedroom, Herb with gun in hand.

When he reached the staircase, he could see four figures coming his way. He pushed Kayla back already knowing who it was. His partner was coming for him. Realizing that he was trapped and outnumbered, he fired a shot in every direction.

BLOCKA! BLOCKA! BLOCKA! BLOCKA!

They returned fire, hitting everything but Herb. They

fired again, this time barely hitting Kayla, who ducked behind the wall.

"You never were a good shot, partner," Herb teased.

"You're gonna see how good of a shot I am, when I get my hands on you, pussy."

An all-out gun battle was in effect, destroying the element of surprise. Gene was tired of the bullshit and ran out the door and around back. He climbed over the gate, in search of a way in. He climbed up to the second floor and through the window. As he made his way inside, he could see Herb's shadow.

Boc! Boc! Boc!

The first slug hit Herb in the back and spun him around. The other slug plunged through his chest. Herb fired back with desperation.

Blocka!

Herb slid down the wall, not able to run. Kayla screamed out, rushing over to Herb. She kneeled down as Gene approached. Merv and his two goons rushed up the stairs to help Gene out. When they made it upstairs, Herb was sitting with his gun still in hand. Merv aimed his gun at Herb's head.

"Put the gun down or I'm gonna finish you right now."

"Please don't hurt us," Kayla begged.

"Shut the fuck up, bitch," Gene said, smacking her across the head with the butt of his gun. She fell beside Herb in pain.

Herb saw this and decided to make a move. He tried to aim his gun, but one of Merv's goons was too quick. He unloaded the clip of the AR-15 into Herb's body. Herb lay against the walk twisted up. Kayla screamed, but Gene gripped her by the hair and pulled her up so their faces were inches apart.

"I'm only gonna ask you one time. Where is my fucking daughter?"

Kayla was hoping that if she told the truth, they would spare her life. As soon as she told him where Tamara was, Gene shot her in the forehead. They rushed to the basement, to find Tamara and DJ on the mattress sleeping. Gene rushed over to his daughter and tried waking her up. He could see the needle marks on her, and knew instantly what they were from.

"Come on, we need to bounce," Merv stated. "The cops are on their way."

Gene grabbed his daughter while Merv grabbed lil DJ, trying to get out of there before the pigs caught up to them. When it came to his daughter, anyone could get it.

EPILOGUE

A lot had happened in the last few months. Tamara was admitted into rehab, where every day was a new struggle for the eighteen-year-old, and Gene made sure he was at every meeting with her. She had endured so much to be so young, but her father made a promise that she would never have to encounter that kind of pain again.

He had taken in DJ as his own, and treated him like his son. They had moved back to Atlanta so he could continue running the businesses he left when he went to prison. He had just dropped DJ off at daycare, and was now pulling up to his construction site. There were some zoning problems at one of his sites, and he needed to get the authorization paperwork for the laborers to continue working. When he pulled up to his office, his parole officer was sitting outside waiting for him.

"Hey, Gene, I was in the area visiting another client, and decided to stop by to check on you. How is the business going?"

"Everything is good, ma'am," Gene said, trying to be polite.

"Okay, well you don't have to report this month since I'm here now. Have a good day, and I'll see you next month," she said, walking away. She stopped all of a sudden

and then turned around. "I have a question for you."

"What's that?" he asked as she walked back toward him.

"Eat my pussy," she said, pushing his head down to her crotch.

Gene eased her skirt up and lifted her up on his desk. They had been fucking for the last month, and she would sneak over to his office once or twice a week. It was one of her fantasies to fuck her parolee, and when Gene was assigned to her, she instantly fell for him.

He knelt between her long legs and clamped his mouth onto her pussy. She was so wet that it dripped all over the papers on his desk. Gene ran his hands up and down her body as his tongue put in work.

"Mmmmm," she moaned, rubbing her titties. "Suck it, baby."

He pushed her knees up closer to her breasts so her pelvis was tilted higher. He could see the crinkled little knot of her asshole in the shadow between her butt cheeks. Gene put his mouth on her crack and pushed his tongue right up her ass before she knew what was happening. No one had ever gone there with her, so it was a whole new experience.

"Holy fuck," she said, in total ecstasy. "Fuck me. I want you to fuck me."

Gene moved up so his dick was lined up with her gaping wet pussy lips, then slid right in without any resistance. She was so hot inside that it felt like his dick was on fire. It got

even hotter when he began pumping in and out of her.

"Oh shit, I'm about to cum," he moaned minutes later, feeling his balls swelling up. No sooner than the words left his mouth, his body jerked and he emptied his clip inside her.

"Finish the job," she whispered, grabbing his head, pushing it back down toward her twat.

He was just sticking his tongue into her musty pussy, when the front door chimed and then opened up.

"What are you doing here?" Gene asked, looking up.

"Sorry, this is personal, not business."

"Wait a minute, let me expla—"

Boc! Boc! Boc!

"Too late!"

COMING SOON:

RETALIATION

Text Good2Go at 31996 to receive new release updates via text message.

BOOKS BY GOOD2GO AUTHORS

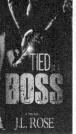

GOOD 2 GO FILMS PRESENTS

WRONG PLACE WRONG TIME WEB SERIES

**NOW AVAILABLE ON
GOOD2GOFILMS.COM & YOUTUBE
SUBSCRIBE TO THE CHANNEL**

THE HAND I WAS DEALT WEB SERIES
NOW AVAILABLE ON YOUTUBE!

THE HAND I WAS DEALT SEASON TWO
NOW AVAILABLE ON YOUTUBE!

THE HACKMAN
NOW AVAILABLE ON YOUTUBE!

FILMS

To order books, please fill out the order form below:
To order films please go to www.good2gofilms.com

Name:_____

Address:_____

City: _____ State: _____ Zip Code: _____

Phone:_____

Email:_____

Method of Payment: Check VISA MASTERCARD

Credit Card#:_____

Name as it appears on card: _____

Signature: _____

Item Name	Price	Qty	Amount
48 Hours to Die – Silk White	$14.99		
A Hustler's Dream - Ernest Morris	$14.99		
A Hustler's Dream 2 - Ernest Morris	$14.99		
Bloody Mayhem Down South	$14.99		
Business Is Business – Silk White	$14.99		
Business Is Business 2 – Silk White	$14.99		
Business Is Business 3 – Silk White	$14.99		
Childhood Sweethearts – Jacob Spears	$14.99		
Childhood Sweethearts 2 – Jacob Spears	$14.99		
Childhood Sweethearts 3 - Jacob Spears	$14.99		
Childhood Sweethearts 4 - Jacob Spears	$14.99		
Connected To The Plug – Dwan Marquis Williams	$14.99		
Connected To The Plug 2 – Dwan Marquis Williams	$14.99		
Flipping Numbers – Ernest Morris	$14.99		
Flipping Numbers 2 – Ernest Morris	$14.99		
He Loves Me, He Loves You Not - Mychea	$14.99		
He Loves Me, He Loves You Not 2 - Mychea	$14.99		
He Loves Me, He Loves You Not 3 - Mychea	$14.99		
He Loves Me, He Loves You Not 4 – Mychea	$14.99		
He Loves Me, He Loves You Not 5 – Mychea	$14.99		
Lord of My Land – Jay Morrison	$14.99		
Lost and Turned Out – Ernest Morris	$14.99		
Married To Da Streets – Silk White	$14.99		
M.E.R.C. - Make Every Rep Count Health and Fitness	$14.99		
Money Make Me Cum Ernest Morris	$14.99		
My Besties – Asia Hill	$14.99		
My Besties 2 – Asia Hill	$14.99		

My Besties 3 – Asia Hill	$14.99		
My Besties 4 – Asia Hill	$14.99		
My Boyfriend's Wife - Mychea	$14.99		
My Boyfriend's Wife 2 – Mychea	$14.99		
My Brothers Envy – J. L. Rose	$14.99		
My Brothers Envy 2 – J. L. Rose	$14.99		
Naughty Housewives – Ernest Morris	$14.99		
Naughty Housewives 2 – Ernest Morris	$14.99		
Naughty Housewives 3 – Ernest Morris	$14.99		
Naughty Housewives 4 – Ernest Morris	$14.99		
Never Be The Same – Silk White	$14.99		
Stranded – Silk White	$14.99		
Slumped – Jason Brent	$14.99		
Supreme & Justice – Ernest Morris	$14.99		
Tears of a Hustler - Silk White	$14.99		
Tears of a Hustler 2 - Silk White	$14.99		
Tears of a Hustler 3 - Silk White	$14.99		
Tears of a Hustler 4- Silk White	$14.99		
Tears of a Hustler 5 – Silk White	$14.99		
Tears of a Hustler 6 – Silk White	$14.99		
The Panty Ripper - Reality Way	$14.99		
The Panty Ripper 3 – Reality Way	$14.99		
The Solution – Jay Morrison	$14.99		
The Teflon Queen – Silk White	$14.99		
The Teflon Queen 2 – Silk White	$14.99		
The Teflon Queen 3 – Silk White	$14.99		
The Teflon Queen 4 – Silk White	$14.99		
The Teflon Queen 5 – Silk White	$14.99		
The Teflon Queen 6 - Silk White	$14.99		
The Vacation – Silk White	$14.99		
Tied To A Boss - J.L. Rose	$14.99		
Tied To A Boss 2 - J.L. Rose	$14.99		
Tied To A Boss 3 - J.L. Rose	$14.99		
Tied To A Boss 4 - J.L. Rose	$14.99		
Tied To A Boss 5 - J.L. Rose	$14.99		
Time Is Money - Silk White	$14.99		
Two Mask One Heart – Jacob Spears and Trayvon Jackson	$14.99		
Two Mask One Heart 2 – Jacob Spears and Trayvon Jackson	$14.99		

Two Mask One Heart 3 – Jacob Spears and Trayvon Jackson	$14.99		
Wrong Place Wrong Time – Silk White	$14.99		
Young Goonz – Reality Way	$14.99		
Subtotal:			
Tax:			
Shipping (Free) U.S. Media Mail:			
Total:			

Make Checks Payable To:
Good2Go Publishing
7311 W Glass Lane,
Laveen, AZ 85339